Praise for JoAnn Smith Ainsworth's
Matilda's Song

"...If you enjoy a good medieval tale, don't miss this one."

~ *ParaNormal Romance*

Rating: 5 Cups "...You will laugh, cry, hold your breath, and cheer with these characters. I found myself pulled right into this story from the first page, and was sad when I realized I had read the last word. Matilda's Song is one of the best books I have read this year."

~ *Coffee Time Romance*

Rating: 4.5 Nymphs "Matilda's Song is a beautiful historic story with scarifies for more than one person and it only got better. ...I thoroughly enjoyed reading this book. ...JoAnn Smith Ainsworth writes of love, mystery and adventure here and the outcome is nothing of what I had even hoped it would be, but a much more rewarding ending."

~ *Literary Nymphs*

Look for these titles by
JoAnn Smith Ainsworth

Now Available:

Out of the Dark

Matilda's Song

JoAnn Smith Ainsworth

A SAMHAIN PUBLISHING, LTD. publication.

Samhain Publishing, Ltd.
577 Mulberry Street, Suite 1520
Macon, GA 31201
www.samhainpublishing.com

Matilda's Song
Copyright © 2009 by JoAnn Smith Ainsworth
Print ISBN: 978-1-60504-323-4
Digital ISBN: 1-60504-195-5

Editing by Bethany Morgan
Cover by Anne Cain

First Samhain Publishing, Ltd. electronic publication: September 2008
First Samhain Publishing, Ltd. print publication: July 2009

Dedication

To my brother, John, and my sister, Carolyn.

Special thanks to Kathy Farrell for the many plot ideas created during our critique brainstorming sessions and Desirae King, whose understanding of motivation added depth to the characters. Thanks to my new critique partner, Julie-Ann Miskell, for suggestions on plot and pacing.

My gratitude to family and friends who believed in me and encouraged me during the early days of this novel.

Chapter One

1120 A.D., Britain

Matilda's heart threatened to escape it was beating so hard. Panic invaded every corner. If Sir Loric discovered her deception, it could be the end of her life. And that of her cousin.

"Hurry!"

She urged her mother and younger sister Nellopa to store the last bundles of clothing and household goods into the wooden cart so she could lash everything down. Her older brother Hylltun and Cousin William were hitching the ox. They kept their voices low and made as little noise as possible to avoid waking neighbors.

"You must be well away from here before Sir Loric knows you're gone," her mother said.

It was nearly midnight in early spring. Matilda and her middle-aged cousin were journeying to his home village of Caelfield where they would live the lie of a newly married couple. They must live this deception until the vindictive knight who demanded her hand to secure his loyalty to the earl saw fit to marry someone else. At eighteen, she was sacrificing all that was familiar to her—family, friends and home village—to evade this knight's attentions.

"You're a saint, William," her mother whispered, "to agree to this sham marriage."

9

"I could never let the family down," he replied matter-of-factly.

When her blacksmith father died last year, the earl invoked his right to choose a husband for her. While the law forbade a lord from marrying a woman to a man beneath her station, it didn't require the husband to be loving, generous or even to her liking. Her skin crawled when Sir Loric just looked at her. He won honors on the battlefield, but off the field he was a lout and a brute.

To escape, she was sacrificing a dream of a love so breathtaking her heart would sing. The lie protected her from a politically motivated betrothal, but it destroyed any prospects of finding and marrying the "man of her dreams"—a reality as bitter and chilling as the night air.

She gave one last tug and tied off the rope securing all her worldly belongings. Her brother—the village blacksmith upon their father's death—finished the harnessing and fed the ox a handful of grain while Nellopa strapped Matilda's most prized possession—a Simple Chest filled with healing herbs—under the cart's seat.

"I'll miss you, Daughter."

Her mother's love reached out and awareness of that loss almost broke Matilda's resolve. She compressed her lips to keep a sob from escaping.

"The earl may never forgive you for this," her older sister said. "It will embarrass him. He may even withdraw my dowry so I can't marry."

Tension built across Matilda's back. She couldn't sacrifice Ingunde's happiness for her own.

"I won't have you hurt. I'll come back if he withdraws your dowry."

"If you return, the earl would have no choice but to give

you to Sir Loric," her brother said.

"Surely, he wouldn't harm Ingunde," their mother assured them. "If for nothing else, to honor his late wife, my dear cousin."

"But he might not let Matilda return to us," Hylltun said, "even if that bastard marries."

Matilda shuddered. She missed her family already and she was not yet gone.

She pulled her cloak closer around her neck.

"The sooner we leave here, the safer I'll feel," William said pragmatically as he took the lead rope and angled the ox toward the moonlit roadway.

Her older sister spoke urgently.

"Go!"

Matilda quickly hugged each one. Her mother's comforting scent of herbs and potions lingered when she tore herself away and caught up with her cousin who was already leading the ox down the rutted lane. Lashed to the cart, her wedding dowry— all her worldly belongings—teetered and wobbled.

As the ox-cart lurched over a large stone uprooted by the spring thaw, she clung with one hand to its wooden side. She looked back, searing her family's shadowed outlines into her memory until the darkness swallowed them.

Chapter Two

Thundering hooves chewed chunks of the packed earth out of the manor house courtyard as the baron brought his enormous, black warhorse to a lurching halt. Lord Geoffrey de la Werreiur of Greystone, Norman baron, knight to the king and ruler of three former Saxon villages, leapt from his lathered stallion, handed off the leather reins to a patient groom stationed nearby and strode briskly toward the entrance of his residence. His white linen tunic stuck to the sweat on his muscular chest.

"Keep riding that hard and you'll break your neck," his elegant sister, Lady Rosamund, admonished from the expansive steps of the manor house. "Then we'll have no heir to continue the de Werreiur line."

Her delicate, beaded, red silk slippers took a beating on the stone pavement, but she insisted on walking outdoors in them.

The baron's brown leather breeches scraped as he rapidly advanced toward the stairs. Knee-high leather riding boots carried the dust of his exploits. His loose tunic flapped wetly in a breeze caused by his rapid strides.

Rosamund thrust her hands onto her narrow hips, a determined expression on her face.

"When are you going to do your family duty and marry? You're almost five and twenty."

Geoff looked at his sister—who probably sought refuge from her domineering husband more than holding a desire to visit her brother.

"You cannot expect me to marry one of those mealy mouthed females you brought with you."

He cringed at the thought of those insipid females, then turned stormy.

"They look at me and calculate the value of my lands. I want a wife who loves me for myself."

Rosamund haughtily defended her friends, her chin rising as she spoke.

"It's their family duty to marry well."

The baron angrily advanced toward the entrance.

"Their eyes glaze over when I discuss the welfare of my tenants. They have no interests except money and fashion."

"You wrong them," Rosamund cried out as he brushed past her to enter the manor through the massive wooden door being held open by a retainer in green and brown livery. "Any one of them can run a manor house."

"I already have an excellent housekeeper," Geoff flung over his shoulder. "I'm looking for a wife. Find me a spirited woman of good birth. Then I'll consider doing my family duty."

"Unrealistic," Rosamund called out as the door slammed shut.

Chapter Three

Two days after they left Wroxton, her cousin—a stalwart, sober man in mud-caked breeches—pointed toward a sturdy cottage—the first to be seen as they rounded a bend in the road.

"Your new home."

"Hallelujah!" The cottage nestled against the backdrop of a forest whose green tones were offset by the interspersed pastels of fruit trees and flowering shrubs. A yellow-green hedge defined the boundaries of the freehold.

She stretched tired limbs and looked around. Although dense forest encircled three sides of the dwelling, lush fields and verdant meadows surrounded the village proper. The rich brown of newly turned earth set off the green shoots of budding crops. Sounds of animals blended with muffled voices of villagers at work.

Despite the long journey, William walked with ease beside the ox. Gray was scattered throughout his dark hair, but his chest was broad and his arms strong from his years as a woodcutter. Matilda treasured the calm assurance of this upright man who had carefully guided the swaying cart upon which rested the accumulation of her past and the hope for her future.

Reserved by nature, he'd been especially withdrawn since

his beloved wife died of the pox many years earlier. It was her mother's hope that her daughter's liveliness would bring William out of himself.

A sparrow—flitting amid sweet-smelling blossoms—caught her eye. She smiled as its wisps of brown were hidden, then revealed among the pink blossoms.

"Look." She pointed excitedly. "A sparrow."

"There are many," he replied matter-of-factly.

As the sparrow flew away, Matilda felt momentarily crestfallen that her cousin wasn't more spirited.

William stopped the ox at the cottage, its walls framed in dark wood against light-colored wattle. In good repair, its steeply sloped roof was fragrant from new thatching. A flowering dogwood beautified its front wall and highlighted the solid wooden door, skillfully planed to fit tightly against drafts.

She swiveled on the rough cart seat to look with satisfaction down the lane to village dwellings set at a distance.

"No nearby neighbors. Less noise and less smell from others living too close. And the barn is separated from the cottage. No straw, no fleas, no stink." "

"The animals have their own dwelling. My wood allotment as Chief Woodcutter made it possible."

William unhitched the ox from the cart, then tied the patient animal to the dogwood tree. His work-roughened hands were half hidden by the delicate white blossoms. He lifted his long-handled axe—carried for protection against robbers—from the cart and set it against the cottage wall, out of reach of the ox chewing contentedly on young grasses. A finch chirped indignantly at him for disturbing its peace among the fragrant blooms.

"There's an untainted spring a short walk down that forest path."

He pointed to a path near the cooking shed.

"Spring water! I'd have gladly walked five miles in Wroxton to get water straight from the ground rather than use our creek."

William chuckled, the sound coming from deep in his throat.

"Aye. I can imagine you making such a nonsensical trip," he said as he checked the ox to see how it had endured the journey. "Give me ale any day. I'll not chance illness on bad water."

Matilda positioned herself to hop down from the cart. Before she could do so, William was there, his lean, strong fingers on her waist, lifting her easily to the ground. She watched him tuck the cloth of his deep blue tunic back into place at his belted waist afterwards with tidy, methodical movements.

"Most kind."

"Come. I'll show you the cottage."

He turned and led the way.

Matilda stepped lightly over the skillfully planed doorsill, noting the solid, four-inch beams framing the wide doorway. William swung open wooden shutters to let in the spring sunlight. A small, central fireplace would heat the room when necessary, releasing its smoke through a loose flap in the sweet-smelling thatching.

"This room is snug enough to shed cloaks inside!" she said.

Matilda strolled about. For all her cousin's somberness, his cottage contained bright patches of color. Decorative pottery sat on the floor and shelves. One large pot contained long branches of pussy willows, dusty from many seasons of standing there. She would get rid of those and put fresh ones in their place. Another held dried, bright-hued straw flowers. Carved, wooden designs, stained in faded colors, hung on the walls. Moving toward a shelf, she picked up a dark green glass goblet, running her fingers over the rippled surface.

"You have many pretty things," she said, her back to William.

"That belonged to Aelswitha's family and came as part of her dowry. Please leave them as she left them. She loved bright things. I keep them in good repair for her."

A shiver passed through Matilda at the realization that he had spoken as if Aelswitha were coming back. She was an intruder. Her arm felt extra heavy as she returned the goblet to its shelf, but she straightened her shoulders. By the time she turned around to face William, a smile brightened her face.

"We had pretty things at home," she said, hoping to divert his attention from his deceased wife. "Because Father worked the forge, we were seldom affected by a bad crop. Someone always needed a tool or a cooking pot and was willing to trade or work for it."

She wandered toward the sleeping area in the large, one-room cottage. "This drapery looks new." Matilda fingered the unbleached, rough wool that had been drawn across to block off the area.

"Yes," he replied gruffly, unease evident in his voice. "I thought you'd want privacy. You may use the sleeping shelf," William said. "I'll sleep out here on mats."

Matilda was struck by his thoughtfulness. She was used to sleeping together in one room with her family, but this was different. Although family, William was practically a stranger.

"Come outside," he said, taking her hand and guiding her

over the threshold.

"The root cellar for storing the vegetables can be reached from both the cooking shed and the back garden. I store the milk, cheese, butter and dried meat there as well. I have a few chickens and a cow. Aelfred the Herder has been taking care of them for me." He pointed. "Over there I grow the herbs. Here the carrots and turnips will be showing soon."

And indeed they would. The surge of spring had come to the land and the young buds could not resist that siren call. She breathed in the fragrant air, filling her lungs with the heady scent of mock orange blossoms, feasting her eyes on the sprightly blooms.

"May I pick some?" she asked as she ran her hand over a branch.

The gentle sadness that characterized William's face since talking about his wife lightened.

"I'll bring water from the spring for them."

"I can do that. Where's the bucket?"

"In the cooking shed."

He indicated the shed with a wave of his hand.

"I'll let Aelfred know I'm home. When I get back, I'll move the ox into the barn and feed the animals. Will you be all right on your own?"

"Don't worry," Matilda assured him, her voice deliberately light-hearted. "After I get water, I'll unpack and get out of these muddy clothes. I'm anxious to settle in."

William drew close to take her hand into his work-roughened ones. He turned it palm up and raised it to his lips to place a tender kiss there.

Matilda flushed.

"Do you think you'll like it here?" he asked quietly.

"Oh, yes!" she said sincerely.

William started walking away.

This was more than she'd hoped for when she resolved to escape from Sir Loric by moving to Caelfield. The cottage was roomy and bright, warm and well furnished. Her cousin was industrious and sensitive. What more could she ask for? And her romantic heart echoed—*what more, indeed.*

Chapter Four

"What's that?" Geoff placed an authoritative hand on the arm of his overseer, forcing him to halt. Although a Saxon, this longtime overseer was also an older, wiser friend. They were traveling a footpath that connected the manor house with the road to the village of Caelfield.

"A woman. Singing." Voernulf spoke quietly. He pointed. "It comes from over there near the spring."

The baron stepped across the path and brushed aside a leafy branch revealing a young woman with gentle curves, flawless skin, emerald eyes and startling strawberry-blond hair. His body responded.

"What a beauty," he whispered. His heartbeat increased dramatically. "If I believed in love coming like a bolt of lightning, I'd say I was struck."

Voernulf was looking at him quizzically and Geoff knew why. He understood family obligation—the only love in his life must be Norman and noble. This woman with her Saxon features and dirt-splattered clothing was obviously neither.

"Who can she be?"

"We're near William the Woodcutter's cottage," Voernulf said. "She must be his new bride."

As Geoff watched, the woman rolled up her sleeves and

removed her hose to reveal trim ankles and shapely calves. His breath caught in his throat. She sighed as she sank her feet into the cool water of the creek created by the run-off from a spring, then leaned forward to splash her legs. The baron felt like a voyeur. Still, he couldn't bring himself to leave her to her privacy.

"If this is his cousin-bride, she's greatly changed," he whispered. "I saw her when she was but twelve. True, her hair was wild like now, but more blond than red. Her features had some beauty, but she was excessively thin and she acted like a boy. No feminine grace."

"She grew up."

The woman tilted her head as if listening. The baron drew back, wondering if she'd overheard. He watched her stand and stare intently over the narrow creek bed. Then she lifted her skirts and started across, hopping from stone to stone.

"She'll slip," Voernulf hissed.

"Not if she's indeed William's cousin," the baron reluctantly replied, admiring her dexterity. "I witnessed her adroitness years ago."

Remembering her courage brought a thin smile of respect.

"How?"

"Some years ago, William accompanied me on a tour of my estates when our forests needed thinning."

"I remember that."

"We passed the night in Wroxton and were relaxing by the river with his relatives. The children were splashing in the water near the bank when a three-year-old stepped too far out and got caught in the current. She went after him and kept the boy above water until some of us could wade in and grab them both."

Voernulf pointed, diverting his attention.

"A kitten in that elderberry bush. She's rescuing it."

"That must be William's bride," he told his overseer, the confirmation driving nails into the coffin of his hopes and giving birth to jealousy. "She has the same urge to rescue the vulnerable she showed in her youth."

Geoff watched the woman step onto a rock at the base of the tree and stretch up, a kerchief wrapped around her hands to protect them from the kitten's claws. She gently grasped the mewing animal and stepped back down.

"Got yourself into trouble, did you?" he heard her scold the black and white ball of fur. "Took on more than you can handle." She held the limp kitten nose-to-nose. "Well, like you, I narrowly escaped a pile of trouble."

As he watched the tabloid unfold as in a trance, an array of emotions he shouldn't be feeling for a Saxon washed through him. Overpowered by lust, his heart contracted in his chest as if hiding from the onslaught of raw emotions.

She set the kitten on the ground and gave it a push on its rear. "Go home to your family."

It circled around behind her and rubbed against her leg. Geoff envied the kitten.

The woman walked about, looking in all directions, the kitten scurrying to stay at her heels.

"Were you abandoned? Nothing looks like your home."

She scooped the little animal into a small pouch hanging from her girdle.

"You'd best come with me or you'll be food for the weasels."

As she re-crossed the creek, Geoff abruptly turned away. Leaving a startled overseer to catch up, he strode rapidly toward the village, putting distance between himself and this woman who evoked roiling emotions.

Chapter Five

William had already returned from Aelfred's by the time Matilda got back to the cottage.

"I found a kitten by the spring."

The agile kitten had scrambled from the pouch and was crawling up her sleeve. William looked indulgent.

"Make a bed for it in the barn. It can make itself useful killing mice."

"The mice would kill it, more likely. It's barely weaned."

"Put it in a rabbit cage at night," he suggested. "Mice can't get in there."

William unhitched the ox from the tree branch to walk it to the barn.

"Coming back from Aelfred's, I met our baron, Lord Geoffrey de la Werreiur of Greystone. He'll be calling here tonight."

"Tonight?"

Her breath caught in her throat.

William nodded. "To pay his respects to my bride."

Unsure that she was ready for this important first social role as William's supposed wife, Matilda's stomach churned.

☙

"Unworthy thoughts."

Geoff chided himself as he meticulously dressed to call on his Chief Woodcutter and the dazzling female he was imagining unclothed.

"I'll make a fool of myself if not careful."

A certain part of his anatomy had a mind of its own.

He was clad simply, but with special care, wanting to make a good impression. "Because she's new to the village and I'm its overlord," he told himself, justifying his careful grooming. Yet, he felt like a cock preparing to strut before a hen.

After putting the female kitten onto a rag bed in a cage, Matilda joined William to empty out the cart. Her pounding heart and churning stomach had settled down somewhat with the ordinariness of the chores. She pushed aside a cloth to reveal a basket packed to the brim with the embroidered bed linens of her wedding dowry.

"See these, William? I learned fine sewing from Mother."

He looked up briefly from the bundles he was grabbing with two strong hands.

"I remember she learned the gentle arts while Lady-in-Waiting to her cousin, Lady Wroxton," he said.

"She taught them to my sisters and me. I could pass for gentry."

Her cousin looked at her sharply.

"Not that I would try," she quickly added. She didn't want William to think she had aspirations above her station.

"Our biggest lack was wood. The King's Forest Act restricted us too much from gathering kindling."

"Wood is part of my payment," he said.

"I'll be able to cook a hot meal every day, instead of only Sunday."

"Not that frequently," William replied as he passed her, carrying another load of goods into the cottage. "I must repair this freehold with that extra allotment and I make things to sell."

There was more to her industrious cousin than her mother had mentioned.

"What things?"

"Stools, benches, walking sticks. Things I can easily carry to the market. You could sell your embroidery there."

William picked up the basket of embroidered linens and took it into the cottage while Matilda sorted out the foodstuffs she'd brought.

"I'll use some of these for tonight's meal."

"We should hurry. The baron may come early."

"I need to clean off this mud," she said.

"I'll pour a basin of water for us."

Matilda appreciated William's thoughtfulness as she took the last armful of dry goods with her into her new home to put them on the shelves, then fetched clean clothing out of the painted chest.

"Will these be all right for you?" She held up a green tunic and brown leggings.

"Fine," William replied. He pulled his soiled tunic over his head and started washing.

When he finished, she took the basin with her behind the curtain. There she washed and put on a light-weight, purple kirtle she thought blended well with the green of William's tunic. The train kept cool air off her legs while the higher hemline in front made it easy for walking. She fastened it at her neck by a bronze brooch—a gift from her parents and one of two brooches that she owned—before fastening a girdle of woven hemp around her waist.

William was settled into a wooden chair with a mug of ale when she finished dressing. The afternoon sun streamed through the opened window, bathing his face with light as his strong hands clasped the earthen mug.

"Tell me about the baron," she said, hoping that by discussing her new overlord she'd reverse the unease, which was again building up.

William scratched his chin.

"Well, he's been running these lands since his parents died in an accident four years ago."

"So sad."

"He's fair. He requires but three days work a week in return for protection and a dwelling. We hope he'll marry soon and start a family. The cousin who'd inherit is a bad landlord."

"I pray he stays well."

"If he has a problem, it's his youth. These Normans are turbulent men, not given to half measures. He moves too quickly and some resist."

She clucked her tongue at such folly.

"The baron is wealthy," William continued. "Along with Caelfield, he controls two other estates and is knight to the king."

Hearing this did not put Matilda at ease. Her heart sounded in her ears again.

"I should put on my silver brooch and cover my hair. I should be more presentable."

Matilda crossed the room to kneel before a carved chest. She removed the bronze brooch that fastened her kirtle at her shoulder and attached an intricately crafted silver one in its place, but her unruly curls were another matter. She actually preferred her hair free. In truth, she resisted anything that bound her. Nervous fingers defeated all attempts to put a net into place.

"Help me," she pleaded. "My fingers won't obey." She stored the bronze brooch then hurried to the table.

William set aside his mug of ale and took the finely knotted net with its bone pins from her trembling fingers.

"Be calm. These visits are a duty."

William pinned one section of the net above her left ear then drew it under and around her hair to fasten it at the other ear with the second bone pin. The netting at last firmly in place, she put a light supper on the table while her cousin leaned back in his chair, looking content.

Matilda willed herself to be calm like William and failed.

Geoff took his time, seeking to resolve his troubled emotions before arriving at the cottage. He walked the path for a second time that day, hoping the physical exertion would relieve the longing ache that had settled in his gut since seeing the Saxon beauty. He fervently prayed the vexing woman was not William's new bride, but a traveling companion or a sister.

That woman has turned me upside down, he thought.

He was angry with himself, but, perversely, excited to stumble so unexpectedly upon a woman who set his blood boiling.

Chapter Six

Darkening shadows licked at the room. Matilda and William sat side-by-side at the table, finishing a meal of cheese and bread, their heads bent toward each other as they talked. A shadow cut between them, blocking the last rays of a sun that had been feebly forcing its way through the open door. Matilda looked up and gasped. The baron had arrived.

Golden rays from the setting sun caused the visitor's thick sandy hair to glow like fire. The elegant lines of a well-trimmed beard in no way detracted from a determined jaw.

Why is he not clean-shaven in the style of the Norman? she wondered. It's strange he should go against fashion.

Why this should be her first thought she didn't know, but the fact that he followed his own inclinations unnerved her.

His face—arrogant-looking with its straight, aristocratic nose—was nonetheless extremely handsome. Laugh lines around his eyes, crinkling in sun-tightened skin, showed him to be a man to take enjoyment out of life. No mustache hid those sensuous lips on which Matilda's gaze unwillingly locked. A warm flush started at her toes and worked its way up her body. The man's seductiveness was too close to that of her dream lover.

I must be careful, she reproached herself.

The baron stood in the doorway, his supple, knee-high

leather boots planted firmly on either side of the wide doorframe. High cheekbones called attention to his intense, gray eyes that seemed to drink in Matilda's face and form. The riveting intensity of his gaze confounded her, making her uneasy.

William rose abruptly so that his chair toppled backward and slammed noisily onto the wide planks of the cottage floor. While he greeted the baron, Matilda uprighted the fallen chair. She stood behind it and nervously grasped its solid wooden back, trying to be inconspicuous, but William gestured for her to come forward.

"This is Lord Geoffrey de la Werreiur." William's voice resonated his respect. "Lord Geoff, this is my bride, Matilda." She noticed the word 'bride' left her cousin's lips easily.

As she reluctantly abandoned the chair's protective barrier to greet the baron, her heart leapt to her throat, allowing no sound to escape. The curtsy she intended to make never happened.

The baron captured one trembling hand in both of his, creating a tormenting prison. While raising it to waiting lips, he gently caressed its smooth skin with an insistent thumb. When at last he placed the inappropriate kiss upon the back of her hand, she didn't wait for release, but tugged, intending to free her hand quickly. Instead, the baron held it securely and pressed the tip of his tongue to her skin as if to explore its elemental nature. At the same time he looked up at her from under lowered lashes with a twinkle in his eye.

He's deliberately tormenting me, she realized.

She tugged harder and freed her hand, her face flushed with embarrassment, her mouth dry and her tongue still unable to utter a sound.

"Welcome to Caelfield." His voice reverberated deeply within her body. He smiled, teeth flashing white against shadow-darkened skin, acknowledging her discomfort, but not consenting to relieve the emotional pressure. "We've met before."

"Surely not, my lord. I would've remembered."

Her voice sounded strange to her.

"You were but twelve. You've grown up."

The caressing voice flowed around her, adding undertones of meaning. She felt wrapped in an encapsulating cocoon, as if William was pushed out and only she and the baron inhabited this world. Totally disarrayed, Matilda turned aside in panic as William pushed a precisely crafted chair in the baron's direction.

"Sit down, my lord. Would you like something to eat?"

The baron sat, declining the offer of food.

William positioned himself against the wall, allowing Matilda to sink gratefully onto the other chair, having first moved it so the stout table created a barrier between the baron and her shaking body.

She put her hands in her lap—rubbing the offended spot with her skirt—and cast her gaze downward. She didn't want to see those teasing eyes, to experience again that first compelling response that put her heart in her throat. She sat, turning her face to the final rays of the sun, and spoke not a word.

The shadows continued to deepen and the sounds from the village to lessen as evening settled in. With her gaze, she traced the outline of first one shadow and then another, on the smooth plank floor. She shifted nervously on the wooden chair.

As the two men talked, Matilda glanced stealthily at the baron and found him staring at her. She quickly looked away.

Time passed and Matilda heard the conversation become

strained. William labored to find topics, while the baron talked haphazardly, seeming not to care. She stole glances to watch a frown—unconnected with the lagging conversation—periodically form on his arresting face.

The level of unease increased, making the atmosphere leaden. William shuffled restlessly.

At last the baron rose. His brows knitted in a deep frown as though some thought not totally to his liking moved around in his head. He shook himself, squared his shoulders and moved toward the door. There he turned. It was at William that he looked and to William that he spoke.

"I demand first night rights."

Matilda felt the color drain from her face. *Droit de seigneur.* The right of the lord to bed the bride on the wedding night. The thought filled her with horror. She would be ruined.

"First night rights?" William questioned hesitantly. "My Lord, we've been married three days."

"First night on the manor land then." The voice was hard and demanding, allowing no dissent. "I'll send my overseer within the hour."

Matilda's hands clenched, her arms rigid at her side. "You cannot, William," she murmured, her voice barely a whisper.

William stared wide-eyed, his own coloring completely gone. His face reflected the tumult surging through his mind. Pain was etched there—and anger—and bewilderment. Then, as if a great burden had been pushed onto his shoulders, so great it aged him by its touch, he bowed his head and said, "Yes, my lord."

"I had to consent," William said after the baron had left the cottage. His shoulders slumped in defeat.

Anger shook Matilda. She gripped the sides of her chair, her breasts heaving from a rage that consumed her.

"Any possible rights he might have as overlord are gone."

"He's a dangerous man to offend."

"That pagan ritual is long abandoned. It takes gall to call these rights back into existence in this day and age."

"The right still lingers."

She gulped deep breaths of air to calm her fury. The pressure building in her head seemed ready to explode. Alluring as this baron was, she rebelled against being forced to give up the virginity she fiercely protected.

"Besides, we're not married."

"To confess it will expose our lie and put you in danger."

Her heart froze. She couldn't return to the clutches of Sir Loric.

William's great height and strength seemed to have shrunk these last minutes while he struggled with the reality of their situation.

"I don't understand what's come over him, but I know he's a good man. He'll be kind."

"Kind!"

The word spat out of Matilda's mouth.

"Kind or cruel, it makes little difference to the woman who doesn't want to be bedded."

She ran agitated fingers through her hair, tugging off the net, the pins dropping unheeded to the plank floor. Released from the confining strands of thread, her hair tumbled wildly about her flushed face. As she spoke, she twisted the yielding net as if wringing an imaginary neck.

"He decided my fate without even looking at me." Her voice

skirted the edge of hysteria.

She flung herself out of the chair. The netting dropped to the floor, soon trampled under uncaring feet. Her kirtle hem swirled around her ankles and cracked like a whip as she spun around to confront William.

"Do you imagine this night will have no effect on us?"

Matilda locked onto his eyes.

"You're letting him ruin me."

"I can't defy him."

His gaze pleaded for understanding. He slumped down onto a chair.

"I've lived here all my life. I'm too old to start elsewhere," William said, wringing his hands.

She stomped her foot on the wooden planks.

"I escaped one arrogant bastard only to fall prey to another. You wouldn't have treated Aelswitha like this. For her you would have fought."

He flinched as if acknowledging the accuracy of her words. Guilt etched his face. His body bowed as if he'd received a heavy blow to the stomach.

Seeing the anguish she caused, her fury wilted. Her angry heart melted as she remembered his sacrifices for the family.

"Oh, William. How I regret that I cause you such pain."

"Hush. This is not your doing."

Matilda paced, less vehemently now, her thoughts racing. She could run again, but where? The baron's arm had a long reach. As did Sir Loric's. Yielding kept her safe, though probably not from wagging tongues.

William stayed silent, watching.

She moved to the table and rested her tousled head on her

arms as sobs racked her body. Hot tears welled up and flowed freely down her cheeks onto the stained wood. The stresses of these past weeks overwhelmed and undermined her.

William drew near and placed a hesitant palm on her back. Matilda felt soothing warmth leave his hand and make its way down to encircle her aching heart, calming and strengthening her, bringing understanding for his pain.

They stayed this way for some time. She wept—softly now—until all her tears were depleted.

After a while, she sighed deeply. A hint of her resignation entered her voice.

"The baron certainly brought on a storm."

William knelt beside her, enfolding her in his arms and resting her head against his steadying shoulder.

Finally, she raised her head. She gazed sadly into her cousin's eyes. "I'll go, William," she murmured. "I will go."

Chapter Seven

"Madness, my lord. Sheer madness."

"Do you think I don't know that?" the baron countered to his overseer, running his fingers through already tousled hair as he paced his bedchamber. He had argued with himself the whole way back to the manor, but no commonsense argument succeeded over his desperate need to hold this woman in his arms.

"You endanger your good standing with the villagers."

"A risk I'm willing to take."

The baron felt as grim as Voernulf looked.

"When I heard myself demanding first night rights, it was as if I were a different man. I couldn't believe I said those words. Yet, I couldn't bring myself to take them back."

"You risk too much for beauty. You've been passionate about women before only to lose interest," Voernulf reminded him.

"None like this woman!"

The baron raised his arms heavenward.

"My gut twists with the thought of betraying a loyal retainer like William. My mind says our union could spell disaster. My body doesn't care."

"There'll be gossip."

The baron nodded curtly. "I'm counting on you to keep this quiet."

"How many of us know?"

"You, Dunavik and Keridwen."

"Keridwen is a tattletale."

"I threatened her if she talks."

"Why bring her in on this folly at all?"

"I am relying on Keridwen to arrange her hair. No one is better. I long to see Matilda dressed as a noblewoman."

The baron shook a defiant fist at the heavens.

"Cruel life. You wrap me in desire for a married woman far below my rank!"

Voernulf was watching the baron warily. Finally, he spoke.

"I'll do as you ask. If I'm not part of this foolishness, matters may get totally out of hand."

The baron nodded somberly.

"You're a true friend. May a merciful God look kindly on my affliction."

The path was narrow and more overgrown than Matilda expected since it was the same one used by the baron when he left the cottage.

They were traveling uphill. The Normans, she knew, built their manors as fortresses, situated on the highest land.

We Saxons favor the mellowness of wood, she thought. The Normans build in rock on top of ugly dirt mounds with muddy moats, spiked outpost fences and thick gates. A Norman fortress sticks out like a sore thumb—a reminder that we're the conquered.

Matilda pulled her drab, woolen cloak tightly about her as

if needing its protection from the conquering Normans.

Bearing a lantern aloft, Voernulf walked first, taking the brunt of the lashings from obstructing branches hidden by dark shadows. Still, each time a branch scratched her, Matilda added one more bone of contention with the baron. He had strong-armed her and William into a corner with no escape. Her blood warmed with pent-up frustration, counterbalancing the chilled night air that had settled in with persistence once darkness had taken over the forest.

According to Voernulf, when the narrow path met the manor road, walking would become easier. Emotionally drained and weary to exhaustion, she found Voernulf's pace and the steep angle of incline arduous. A thin layer of perspiration dampened her face.

"We're taking this shortcut rather than the road in order to bypass the village," he had explained. "The baron wants to keep your visit from inquiring eyes."

Self-pity welled up within her. After tonight she would be living two lies, one of her own making and one brought about by the baron.

Woody tips of branches and sticky brambles caught at her dark-hued skirts. Although a full moon shone in the clear sky, its light was frequently hidden by the dense, dark branches. The birds and animals common to a nocturnal walk were unseen and unheard tonight. Seemingly, Nature herself had turned away from Matilda, refusing to acknowledge her passage or to give her succor. As the confining branches closed behind her, cutting off retreat, her battered spirit experienced the closing off of all her plans and dreams, leaving only the dark unknown.

The overgrown pathway suddenly burst upon a broad, well-cared-for thoroughfare rimmed on either side by thick forest.

The roadway curved to the right, disappearing into dense foliage. Here the full moon gained complete power and bathed everything in gleaming luminescence. An owl hooted, the sound carrying clearly in the still night.

Voernulf stopped and turned to Matilda. "You're tired," he said, scrutinizing her face, frowning at her evident exhaustion.

"Yes."

He put an arm under her shoulders, giving welcomed support. "Come. We're almost there."

As they rounded the last bend, Matilda abruptly stopped, causing Voernulf to jerk to a halt. Her mouth fell open in amazement. Before her stood, not the Norman eyesore she expected, but a Great Hall in the Saxon fashion, its magnificent dimensions and delicate balance of construction a pleasure to the eye. Massive grey stone walls rose in the moonlight to a height that rivaled the trees of the forest, yet remained in perfect symmetry with them. The roadway curved and circled in front of the structure with smaller pathways breaking off to wind enticingly around either side. Laurel blossoms, growing on well-tended trees, festooned the front of the manor house, softening the effect of the massive stone walls. Meadow, well trimmed by the goats in residence there, provided a pastoral setting. No fortress this, despite these walls, but a gracious dwelling of considerable proportion.

"What is it?" Voernulf watched her anxiously. "Is something wrong?"

"No, I'm all right," Matilda responded, recovering her composure. "I expected a fortress, not a manor in the Saxon style with tended fields and flocks. Norman interest is claimed by war. It's we Saxons who love the land and cattle."

"This baron is different," Voernulf said, his voice swelling with pride. "His parents fortified the Saxon Great Hall with field stone, but that's all they did. No muddy moats, no spiked fences here."

He took her hand.

"Come. Let's finish this journey."

Silently, they walked the remainder of the roadway. They moved past the fragrant laurels along the smaller pathway that led to the rear entrance of the manor.

No front door treatment for me, she thought.

The massive door swung inward, revealing a matronly Saxon woman in a dark brown gown with a coif covering her graying hair. The veil of her coif was pinned to conceal an aging neck. The woman reached out to take Matilda's free hand securely into her own warm grasp. Voernulf released her other hand, moving away. As the door closed, something meaningful went out of her life. When she left this mansion, she would no longer be an innocent.

"I'm the housekeeper, Dunavik."

Stepping back into the hallway, the woman urged Matilda farther into the corridor before holding her at arm's length to look at her closely.

"I don't agree with him, as well he knows, but I'll do my best to make you comfortable."

Her manner was that of a mother whose favorite son could do no wrong, even if she had doubts about his present conduct.

"You look exhausted, my dear." She gathered Matilda into her large bosom and planted a motherly kiss on her cheek.

The chatelaine of a Norman household normally would be Norman, not Saxon. Also, Matilda expected the baron's chatelaine, in charge of the servants and the general functioning of a large manor where no mistress was installed, to be domineering, not plump and motherly.

Why is so much about this baron surprising? she wondered.

"Follow me, dear," Dunavik said. "Don't dawdle."

With that, she entered a stone corridor stretching toward the innermost reaches of the manor.

A reluctant Matilda followed. Her voluminous, heavy wool cloak clung tightly to her legs as if to coerce extra effort from her. Her wooden clogs echoed on the freshly cleansed flagstones.

Dunavik led the way down the dimly lit passageway off which branched the kitchen, several pantries and various storerooms. The general clatter and bustle of the evening meal was long past, but stale aromas still lingered. It was obvious this was the servants' portion of the manor. Dunavik, seemingly at ease under these strange circumstances, chatted about the comings and goings of the manor.

"Lord Geoff's mother, God rest her soul, set up the routine for this household, and I saw no need to change it. His father planned the additions to the Hall," she continued, seemingly unaware of the turmoil raging inside Matilda, "but he died too soon. Lord Geoff finished that work. This new section is built of rock. Less chance of fire from the kitchens."

Dunavik's voice bounced off the stone walls as they passed.

"The tapestries in the main rooms are a wonder. Most of them were brought by ship from Flanders. And they have the very best examples of carved Italian chests and Viking brass and iron ornaments."

She halted before a solid, unadorned door near a back stairway and Matilda held her breath. When Dunavik turned, she evidently saw her distress because she said soothingly, "This is not the baron's chamber."

A sense of reprieve flooded through Matilda as Dunavik opened the door and ushered her into a good-sized bathing room. With eyes blurring—as much from tears of relief as by the moisture in the room—she surveyed her surroundings. An iron cauldron hung in a small hearth built into one corner provided hot water and added warmth and moisture to this stone chamber.

Matilda had heard that indoor commode rooms were gaining in popularity, but a bathing room was almost unheard of, even though the hated Romans had left tiled baths and steam rooms. The nobility still used washing basins, not tubs. Or, for men and boys, the trough in the courtyard.

The large, wooden barrel tub commanded Matilda's attention. Round and mid-thigh height, its wooden interior had a bench to allow the bather to rest contentedly shoulder-deep in heated water. From the alluring scent rising from the moist, hot steam, she deduced that fragrant rose petals had been added.

A wooden stool stood near the tub to aid the bather getting in and out. Matilda realized the plug at the bottom of the tub must release the used water into the drainage ditch, allowing it to flow past a flap in the wall to drain outside, much like the drainage used in the commode rooms.

To carry the water needed to fill such a tub was an extravagance beyond Matilda's dreams and said something about the baron's sense of cleanliness and his wealth.

Candles burned on the wooden shelf built above a large, ornately carved chest set against the far wall. The candles cast a warm glow, filling the room with soft, flickering light. Jars of oils and fragrances, prominently displayed on the shelf, released sweet aromas as warm, moist air caressed her, weaving its spell of self indulgence and wellbeing.

"This is the baron's own bathing room," Dunavik said,

continuing her monologue. "You must be special to be using it."

"More likely he wants the grime from my journey gone before he touches me," Matilda said sarcastically.

Dunavik ignored the remark, opened the ornate chest and casually held up a large cloth. "You can dry yourself with this."

Matilda couldn't draw her astonished eyes away from the scarlet drying cloth Dunavik held. Soft, of finely woven linen, it would be a luxury, even for a queen. Its size, to Matilda, seemed enormous.

When Dunavik turned her back to reach again into the carved chest, Matilda furtively picked up the cloth from the wooden stool on which it had been casually dropped and pressed it against her cheek. Its smooth, soft texture excited her senses. Guiltily, she dropped the cloth as the chatelaine started talking.

"Here are the garments you'll wear for the evening." Dunavik pointed to folded habiliments on top of a chest. "A serving girl will be along to dress your hair."

She turned to leave the room, but paused at the doorway and added, "Don't dally, my dear. The baron will be waiting."

"Don't dally," Matilda fumed aloud at the closed door. "Don't delay the baron's pleasures. But first a bath. As if I stink."

Her indignation rose to new heights.

"I'm as careful about my person as the nobility."

She started pacing, arms stiffly at her side, hands clenched tightly into fists.

"They want to wash and dress me like a prize fowl for the plucking."

She'd resist! Her lips compressed into an angry line. Back

and forth she stomped, her mind awhirl.

Slowly reality sank in. She stopped pacing. Her proud shoulders drooped.

"If I don't obey, I destroy any chance William and I have for a life in Caelfield."

She sighed deeply and started to undress.

"It's only one night."

Her fingers felt awkward and clumsy as she released the clasp of her dark-colored cloak and hung it on a wall peg. She looked down at the dress she wore with chagrin. Earlier, she had changed from her purple kirtle into drab, gray wool. She had thrown a dull, hooded cloak over her shoulders and head, pulling its drawstrings tight to close off the brilliantly colored hair whose unruliness and fine texture so much expressed her personality. She'd told herself grumpily at the time, "I have to go to the manor. I don't have to make my person a delight for him."

The baron had thwarted her even in this.

She walked to the chest. A linen undergarment was placed on top of a blue outer garment, effectively hiding it from her view. Matilda reached under to pick up the blue gown and shake it out, curious to see what she was to wear.

"Ahhh!"

Stunning yards of cerulean blue unfolded and fell tumbling to the floor revealing a gown of lightweight, loose-woven wool that must have been created by a master seamstress. Matilda's eyes devoured every aspect of the breathtaking gown.

Luxurious gray-white fur rimmed a neckline that would dip to reveal an expanse of slender white throat and upper bosom. Long sleeves, carefully tailored to cling lovingly to shapely flesh, tapered to a point at the back of the hand to enhance long, beautiful fingers. Its demi-train, by accentuating height, would intensify a regal bearing. The elegant blue color deepened in tone in the folds of the full skirt, to cause a kaleidoscope of changing hues as the wearer moved.

Eyes closed, she hugged the gown, envisioning herself enfolded in its lovely embrace. Wrapped in fantasy, she swayed gracefully in sybaritic dance on the flagstone floor, her enthralled spirit responding innately to the sensuousness of the gown. Transported, she fled in fantasy to a royal banquet where, wearing this spectacular dress, she was the envy of all who saw her. And holding her tightly in his arms was the royal prince—handsome, cultured, rich, looking very much like...

"No!" Matilda froze. It was not a dream prince who would hold her, but the baron. And this gown did not belong to a fantasy from which she could awaken, but a reality from which she could not escape. The man for whom this dress was intended was not a husband. Yet, he would hold her and make love to her, and she could say neither "yea" nor "nay". A pain rent her breast. She dropped the gown in a heap on the chest, a tear slipping from her eye.

Sadness invaded her as she shed her remaining clothes, stepped onto the stool, and then dutifully into the tub. As she settled into the water, its soothing warmth closed around her, wrapping her in a cocoon of enervating luxury.

With a sigh, she lowered herself totally into the sweet-smelling water and rested her head against the tub's welcoming rim.

Fears momentarily forgotten in the experience of being shoulder deep in heated water, a smile settled on her lips and her eyes closed as if in a light doze. She stayed this way for some time, her body totally at ease.

"If only he were less attractive."

She tried to convince herself that she was making more of the circumstances than they warranted. The memory of insistent lips pressed to her skin brought disturbing tingles, leaving her shaken.

"I grew up too stiff necked. If I were like some women, I'd enjoy this night with no conscience to disturb me."

But an exciting partner for one night was not for her. She wanted to share life every day with a man she cherished.

Agitated, she shifted position uneasily, the water making tiny lapping noises as she moved. Its rose scent invaded her troubled thoughts.

Matilda spoke to the empty room. Her words were absorbed in the cooling steam.

"I must come out of this night with my pride intact."

She mulled over ways to thwart him without jeopardizing William.

Suddenly, she straightened in the tub.

"His need shall be my weapon against him. I'll find the chink in his powerful armor. In his need rests my strength."

This knowledge invaded her like a light to a dark cavern. Her lips curled in a smile that bordered on a gloat.

Relieved, she closed her eyes languidly, allowing herself to experience the caress of the water. The warm, scented bath relaxed her, working the stiffness out of her muscles. Two days on a jolting cart had taken their toll.

"A pity I can't stay like this forever."

She lifted a handful of the scented liquid and allowed it to drip slowly through her fingers onto her bare arm. Delighting in the sensation, she did it again before taking up the washing cloth. She ran it lightly over her face and neck and down her water-softened skin as though its touch had the power to heal the pains of her spirit.

A sharp rap on the door startled her. A brusque voice said it was time to dress.

Reluctantly, she climbed out of the tub. She wrapped the scarlet bath linen completely around herself, feeling the soft fabric against her naked skin.

Walking to the shelf, she chose lilac-scented oil and applied it. Her hand slid easily, coating her warmed skin with a fragrant film. Fragrances from the bottled oils invaded her senses. The aromas reminded Matilda of the softening oils her mother made, herbal formulas she now possessed. The soft texture of her skin attested to the moisturizing qualities of her mother's mixtures used since early youth.

"If his need is to be his defeat, I'll need all the attraction I can muster from this fragrance."

Satisfied with the effect of the oil, she moved to the chest and lifted the linen undergarment off the carved surface to slip it over her head. The superfine linen cascaded around her, sweeping the floor with a rustling sound. Matilda settled the delicately woven material over her breasts and tugged it into place around her waist. It felt magnificent compared to her own rough wool undergarments. Cloth ties fastened it together at bosom, waist and skirt. She donned linen leggings that would protect her from the cold of the night, then wiggled into a pair of beaded, blue slippers.

She had only just settled the soft fabric of the blue gown about her body when the door burst open. A servant, a few years older than Matilda, barged in.

"I'm Keridwen. I'm here to do your hair, but by the looks of it there's little I can do."

She flounced about the room gathering brushes and combs.

Matilda wondered how this servant could be so deliberately impertinent, but it was a fleeting thought. She had more pressing worries.

"Please, do me no favors."

"I wouldn't," the woman said with a swish of fulsome hips, "but the baron will be furious if I don't make some attempt."

The servant ushered her to the small stool by the chest and started to brush. As tangles were removed and ribbons added, the inevitability of the night crept in, restricting Matilda's breathing. She'd never lain with a man.

"You have no business being here," the woman said. "You're Saxon and no better than me."

"My being here is none of my doing. Your quarrel is with the baron, not with me. I'm a married woman."

She wasn't going to let these people forget she held status as wife to William, even if based on a lie.

Before the servant could snap out a reply, Dunavik knocked and entered.

"Are you done, Keridwen?"

"Almost," the servant replied with considerably more respect than she'd shown Matilda. With a few more sweeps of the brush, she brought the last strands under control around Matilda's face and placed the final ribbons.

"Stand, my child," Dunavik commanded.

Matilda stood.

With a tug here and a pull there, the chatelaine settled the lush fabric more evenly, then stepped back.

"My gracious, but this color is becoming. It brings out your hair and your eyes."

Admiration shown as clearly on her face as resentment was etched on Keridwen's.

"Follow me."

Dunavik opened the door and left the room.

Matilda's feet refused to obey. They stayed rooted to the bathing room floor.

"Go on."

Keridwen gave her an ungentle push.

She swallowed deeply and left the room. Her heart pounded in her ears.

Dunavik led the way a short distance along the corridor, then up narrow back stairs lighted here and there with torches. Matilda watched her placid bulk ascend as if nothing untoward were occurring.

The stairs ended at a wooden door, plain on the stair side but carved in rose patterns once they stepped through into a wide, upper hallway. The carved pattern opulently lined the long hall, while portraits and tapestry decorated its walls. When Dunavik slowed, a pounding pressure built in Matilda's head. Her knees felt weak.

The chatelaine stopped at the carved door dominating the end of the corridor. There she knocked.

"Enter," a deep voice called out.

Dunavik opened the door and gently pushed Matilda into the baron's chamber, shutting the door securely behind her.

Chapter Eight

Matilda's heart missed several beats when she looked at the huge, intricately carved oak bed centered between two large, shuttered windows. She swallowed—or tried to, but found her mouth suddenly dry. Flickering candles created an enticing den for luring prey. Several comfortable looking, leather-backed chairs were scattered about. The baron was sitting on one of these chairs before an ornamented fireplace where a fire glowed with a steady blaze.

He emerged from his chair, seeming to grow taller as he rose. Matilda envisioned his encroaching presence expanding until it filled the entire chamber, smothering her. She shivered, both at the trap she had walked into and, perversely, at the undeniable appeal of this man.

Every noble inch of him bespoke power. His resplendent silk tunic was a vivid green embroidered with bands of gold at neckline and sleeve edge. Worn opened at the neck, it revealed a golden medallion on a heavy chain nestled in a mat of sandy hair. His face as he came toward her carried a curious blend of relief and desire. Tension fairly crackled in the air. His muscles rippled, emphasizing the earthy manliness of him. The effect was nearly her undoing and she tried to recall the resolutions she'd made in the bathing room.

Lord Geoff stood before her, one hand outstretched.

"Come."

She must place her hand in his—must allow herself to be entrapped—to fulfill her part of the bargain.

Ah, William, she bemoaned, how could you abandon me to this?

Into a richly furnished web he drew her, like a fly to an enticing, deadly spider. Geoff gathered her against his muscled body and bent to kiss her lips deeply, fully, seeming to draw sustenance from the depths of her. She felt a tremor move through him and echo in her own body.

He slowly released her.

"I have mulled wine and dried fruit. Sit with me awhile by the fire. Eat."

The feminine wiles, which seemed her defense while soaking in scented water, never materialized. Instead, the confusion of innocence rose up. She'd never before experienced such sensations. They paralyzed her, constricting her breathing and creating a loud roar in her head. She could do nothing more than place her fingertips on his arm and walk with him to the fireplace.

She slipped down onto a chair and gratefully rested her shoulders against its leather back. Her knees were trembling and her fingers nervously roamed the fabric in the skirt of the blue gown. She was drowning in an experience beyond any she had known or could even imagine.

"Eat," he again urged her so she reached out for the mulled wine. The swallow she hoped would relieve her parched throat failed abominably and she returned the golden goblet to the table before the wine spilled from her shaking hands.

"I can't."

Her voice didn't sound like her own.

"Do you want music? Shall I call the musicians?"

She shook her head, not trusting a sound to come out.

Her friends had gossiped about the lustiness of love, but they failed to expose the power of its attraction, a mystical appeal that consumed and had a mind of its own. Any resistance she had planned no longer had meaning.

He drew her to her feet to kiss her. His enfolding arms tightened as the kiss deepened. All the breath of life seemed to be draining from her body. Surely, she must be a shell of her original self. She tried without success to ruthlessly quell the sensations welling in her loins.

Her heart pounded in her ears as he lifted her to carry her across the room to the oak bed. Its red draperies were pulled back, tied in readiness to drop into place to keep out the night's cold air.

Gently, he placed her on the high bed. He removed one beaded slipper and then the other. "You are my torment."

"How strange," Matilda replied, "for you are mine."

His hands moved with confidence, removing her linen stockings, which he dropped on the beaded slippers to make a pile on the floor. Without success, she tried to pull away from his exploring hands, which had reached the fastenings at her bodice and become insistent.

In a tortured voice he said, "Fate drove desire deep into my heart the moment I saw you."

He pushed the lush blue garment aside, pressing his lips to her exposed flesh, raining sweet kisses from her neck to her breasts. His beard left prickly imprints on her agitated skin. He maneuvered the splendid gown off her shoulders and pulled away the tapered sleeves with impatience. The ministrations of Dunavik and Keridwen were rapidly destroyed. His habiliments joined hers on the floor.

Matilda felt exposed, vulnerable. She rolled on her side to move away, but found herself relentlessly pulled back as Geoff joined her on the bed and stretched his long form beside hers. His hands roamed her body and nestled in her abundant hair. The weight of him pressed her deep into the goose down mattress. Their limbs entwined as if nature had intended it so.

"Tonight, I am determined to dig you out of my soul."

The heavy bed drapes hadn't been pulled to keep out the night's chill, and the coolness brought relief to their overheated bodies. Their murmurs were the only sounds drifting into the night.

The male scent emanating from him heightened her tension, increased the yearning. She gave up any ideas of resistance and floated on a cloud of mounting sensation. He was like a lodestone, inexorably drawing her, draining her of resolve. She betrayed herself in his arms.

"I'm lost."

Matilda moaned this drowning thought as waves of ecstasy washed over her.

All thoughts of resistance—all worries and fears—melted away. The secret of her virginity she was protecting—her sham marriage—was about to be exposed and she cared not a jot. Tomorrow would heal itself. Tonight was hers for love.

With joy, she gave way to that which she would no longer resist. All thought of what should have been or what might have been evaporated. Moist, ready, only her need had reality. And Geoff, sensing her desire, chose that moment to blend his need with hers.

The night was long, but by the time of their slumber, they had known each other again, and then again.

Chapter Nine

Sunshine burst through the windows as Dunavik banged the shutters open. The sounds of meadow birds joined the sun in proclaiming the new day.

"Rise, my dear. Everybody has been up and about for hours."

Dunavik's buoyant good cheer was almost more than Matilda could bear. Her head was buzzing. Her body felt strange and seemed not her own.

"I've brought you some food to break your fast. It's on the table. Your clothes are on the bench," the chatelaine said as she bustled about putting the room to order.

"I don't want food. I want to go home."

Mention of her clothes made Matilda conscious that she was naked under this bedding.

Memories of the past night invaded—his hands, his mouth, the breathless agony of pleasure drawn from her depths.

She ruthlessly pushed out all thoughts and shut her mind's door. At some point she'd think about last night, but not now. She wasn't ready.

Today's realities were her wool shift and gray gown. On the floor waited her stockings and walking shoes from yesterday. The dull cloak hung by the wardrobe. The exquisite gown and slippers had disappeared—as had Geoff.

Matilda noticed she used his first name in her thoughts. To the outside world he would be "Lord Geoff", but in her inner world he would be her "Geoff", the man of her dreams.

His absence was a bitter pill.

Reality hurt and froze her heart. Her dream lover was lost to her. He was noble and Norman. She was Saxon and supposedly married.

"Now to put my life back together," she said to the room, forgetting that Dunavik was still there.

"You can be certain of my discretion. Voernulf's too. He'll show you to your cottage."

"I'll find my own way."

"Are you sure?"

Matilda vigorously nodded her head.

"I want nothing to remind me of last night."

"If you insist."

"I'd like to get dressed."

"Certainly, child. I'll be back in a little while."

Dunavik left, taking the uneaten food with her.

Slipping out of the bed, Matilda donned her own drab garments. When dressed, she sat on a carved, wooden bench by the window and waited, her body weighted down with hopelessness as heavy as lead. The songs of the birds coming through the unshuttered windows seemed distant and unreal. She found herself wishing she'd eaten the meal Dunavik had laid out for her. She sat listlessly, finding it hard to summon up the energy needed to resume her life. After what seemed an interminable time, Dunavik reappeared, saying, "If you're ready, my dear, I'll show you out of the manor."

"I'm ready." She rose to follow the chatelaine, leaving the fateful bedchamber without a backward glance. What would it serve to look back and imagine a different ending? What would soothe the empty region where her heart had been?

The wall tapestries appeared even more dramatic in the bright rays of the morning sun than in the flickering candlelight of last night. Matilda passed them with barely a glance, eager to leave the manor and all its trappings behind.

She followed Dunavik down the narrow staircase, through the corridors and past the kitchen. When another sigh passed Matilda's lips, Dunavik said, "Try not to be bitter, dear. You're young. This madness will be forgotten over time."

"I don't know if I can ever forget."

They had reached the final door, which Dunavik opened cautiously. She quickly pressed her cheek to Matilda's. "Take care of yourself, child."

Matilda stepped into the freedom of the sunshine as Dunavik closed the heavy door. She took a deep breath. Finches twitted excitedly overhead. She puzzled over what had disturbed them, causing them to complain, when she caught movement at the corner of her eye. A disheveled William stepped from the brush, looking haggard and drawn.

"William!"

Matilda took his outstretched hands in hers. As she touched him, the pent-up emotions of last night broke free and tears streamed down her face. She had glimpsed a distant dream of love, grasped it last night with all the fervor of her being and tore it from her heart this morning. The hollowness left behind pained as nothing she had ever experienced except the death of her beloved father.

"Are you all right?" he asked, urgently.

"I hope I will be. For now, I don't want to talk."

William nodded.

"I'll take you home."

He stepped in front of her to lead the way down the path, being careful to keep protruding branches well out of her way.

The joys of last night and the pain of today's separation washed over her as she concentrated on how to put one foot in front of the other. To negotiate the pathway in daylight with a mind in turmoil seemed as hampering as traveling it in the darkness of the night. Gradually, she became aware of the hunched shoulders and tousled appearance of her cousin.

"You look terrible, William."

"I stayed out here all night," he answered over his shoulder. "I didn't want you to be afraid if the baron had sent you home at night."

Matilda couldn't speak for a moment. She was tongue-tied by William's sacrifice. Guilt leaked into her heart. While she was lost in love in Geoff's arms, William waited alone in the cold.

"How glad I would have been to find you there, William," she said softly. "How truly glad."

They made a slow journey of it, but eventually arrived at their home. This was the place she had run to for refuge. This must be the place to begin anew.

Matilda expected to see some remnant in the cottage of the emotional storm that preceded her departure. She saw none. The morning sun poured in the open door, drawing shifting patterns on the carefully planed wooden floor. William seated her solicitously at the table. He brought nuts and milk, behaving as if there had been no interlude at the manor. Each carried guilt. Each had reasons to forget. Matilda saw that forgiveness underlay their good manners.

"Would you like something else?" he inquired when she'd finished.

"No. I'm more tired than hungry."

Her exhaustion was an emotional drain not easily undone by sleep. Although she slept last night, she needed desperately to replenish herself emotionally. She needed strength to resume her life of lies.

"We'll both rest," William said as he led her to her bed, abandoning the dirty dishes on the table without a backward glance. Drawing back the curtain separating her sleeping area from the main room, he allowed Matilda to precede him as they climbed onto the bed to lie, fully clothed, on top of the bedding. Matilda turned her back to him and folded easily into the length of his body. William wrapped his arms around her and placed his chin on the top of her head, holding her close. She fell asleep feeling comforted and secure.

"Coward," the baron condemned himself. "Bastard."

He had sneaked out of the bedchamber in the early hours, leaving a sleeping Matilda to face the new day alone. He feared that he might never let her go if he lingered.

Geoff granted his eager black charger its head, recklessly galloping across his meadowlands. Caring nothing about direction, his only demand of the powerful mount was speed.

As they raced on, the baron berated himself. He was bewitched with an unsuitable woman—married, Saxon and of mediocre birth.

And she'd been a virgin. When his woodcutter said they were married three days, Geoff assumed the marriage was consummated. His joy at finding he was her first lover was profound.

He ruthlessly quelled his turbulent emotions. In his position, he couldn't afford the indulgence of love.

Duty created an impossible barrier. He headed an important family. People depended on him for their livelihood and protection. They looked up to him as an example. His life was not his own—it belonged to his family, his king and his tenants.

Geoff jabbed his lathered horse in the ribs, coaxing more speed out of it.

Arriving home hours later—physically and mentally exhausted—he found himself just as uncertain as when he'd left the manor that morning about how to act honorably and achieve a quiet heart while Matilda was only minutes away from his touch.

Matilda awoke first, feeling somewhat refreshed. She extricated herself from William's arms and crawled stealthily from the bed. Looking back, she saw his face was less haggard. Sleep was healing him.

Ignoring the abandoned food still set out on the table, she took a chair into the garden to let the early afternoon sun warm her face. The fragrances of the forest teased her nose as she willed herself into forgetfulness. She sat like this for a long time and then aroused herself to start her chores.

"I might as well get started on this new life of mine."

As she approached the cooking shed, she noted it shared the same careful construction as the cottage.

"That's my cousin. Each piece fitted perfectly into place."

The hide covering on the doorway kept the bad weather out—a more usual covering on most homes than the door

William had mounted on his cottage. Situated so that their dwelling would not easily catch fire should an ember escape while cooking, this shed was yet not so far away that it would be a burden keeping the food hot for the table.

Matilda's eyes adjusted to the dark coolness inside. Her gaze met more abundance than to be expected in an end-of-winter larder. Wicker baskets overflowed with potatoes, dried fruit and herbs. Jugs and baskets held other stores. "William must do well bartering in the marketplace." She'd have a physically comfortable—if emotionally precarious—life in Caelfield.

Iron pots hung on hooks at either side of a large fireplace on the far wall. Platters and eating utensils were stacked neatly on shelves. An old storage chest had Germanic runic inscriptions carved on its side. Matilda wished she'd been taught to read and write this language, which might die out under Norman rule. New words were already corrupting it. Most scholars today had forgotten these runic characters and relied on Latin. With French spoken at the court and Latin spoken in the ever-increasing Christian churches, the Old English tongue was losing ground.

She stepped back out into the bright sunshine to absorb the earthy smells of the garden. Her young spirit responded to the sunlight and she cleared the table and washed the dishes. She fed the animals, then released the kitten from her cage and carried her to the chair in the back garden. While absorbing the sun's soothing warmth, she petted the black and white kitten as she lay curled in her lap.

"Enjoy your innocence while you can," she told her. "Once males take an interest in you, life becomes treacherous."

She dropped her voice to a whisper.

"Last night I found my heart's desire."

The petting became erratic as increasingly strong waves of despondent emotion washed through her.

"My mother used to say, 'Be careful. You might get what you wish for.'"

A single tear ran down her cheek.

"Now, I understand. My dream man turned out to be a Norman lord. There's no honorable future for me with him. My duty is to William who keeps me safe from the clutches of Sir Loric. If a child comes from last night, I'll raise it Saxon."

Her father had been a respected member of the woten, the village council of wise men. Proud of their Saxon heritage, it had been terrible for him to watch the dismantling of the kingdoms of Engla lande and see *Regia Anglorum* rulers replaced by Normans. Even the Anglo-Saxon common sense rules were overshadowed by Norman rulings.

"It could be worse," William had said as they journeyed to Caelfield. "When King Henry married a Saxon noblewoman, some of our Saxon Folk Rights were restored. We at least have equality under the law, even if we're not considered equal in social standing."

"Yes," she decided, emphatically, "a child will know my heritage. Its father abandoned us. He left before first light without a word, his need satisfied. If the child looks like Geoff, well, it wouldn't be the first time that an overlord had his way."

The kitten squirmed and dug one sharp claw into her leg. With a yelp, she pushed her from her lap. As it scampered away, she called after it. "I name you 'My Fate'. You bring me pain along with joy."

She spent the rest of the afternoon working in the garden and gouging out all emotion by locking up her heart.

When William awoke late afternoon, Matilda came inside the cottage. His hair was tousled and his clothes crumpled. She put her arms around his waist and laid her head on his chest.

"Never mention last night," she said flatly. "Pretend it never happened."

"We can try," William responded, "but it'll come out when we get angry."

"Let's wait until that time."

Chapter Ten

Despite her reluctance, William had convinced her it was best to meet his friends and neighbors rather than hiding away. As they walked to the center of the village that evening, he distracted her from her worries with its history.

"Caelfield is an old village, founded by the Celts. We Saxons claimed it six generations ago. Now we have Norman overlords."

Matilda well understood the loss of worldly status suffered by the Saxons after the Battle of Hastings.

"Caelfield is larger than the Domesday Book records give us credit for," William informed her. "This manor is recorded with a mill, fishing and land for seven ploughs. We extended the farmland these past years and it never got counted in the Book."

Matilda observed that Caelfield had a level landscape, more easily adapted to laying out fields and common lands of equal size. Her girlhood home of Wroxton was a high-wold village of rolling plains and lay closer to the coast. The flatness made their walk tolerable after the rigors of yesterday's ox-cart journey. As Matilda walked along, she spotted deer at the boundary of a meadow edged by forest.

William spoke of the last time the peasants were called to arms. "No training of thanes for war takes place in Caelfield now," he told Matilda. "That training is done at Drengham, where the lesser nobles live. The storehouses and the town hall for justice are built there as well. When we Anglo-Saxons ruled, our kings would stay at Drengham when it was the scheduled time to visit the district or to collect the taxes."

As they drew near the first homes of the village proper, William hailed a heavily bearded man of tremendous upper body breadth and muscle development. Matilda braced herself to meet her first neighbor.

"This is Stowig, the finest smithy for miles around."

She greeted the blacksmith, feeling as if she was on display.

"It's good to see you returned safely. Your bride is a beauty." Stowig put a brawny arm over William's shoulders. "You flatter me with your introduction. You must want something."

"Nothing for me, but I would be pleased if your good wife would take Matilda under her wing, to help her settle in."

"Easily done," Stowig said. "We'll go now."

They crossed the wide road and entered a cottage not as comfortable as William's, but nonetheless roomy and well furnished. Inside, a slender woman of middle years in a dark brown garment turned to greet them.

"What's this, Stowig?" she asked, her eyes twinkling. "You leave your job before day's end?"

"I brought William's bride to meet you," he said. "Matilda, this is my darling wife, Berwyn."

"You are lovely," she said as she clasped Matilda's hands. She turned to William. "I hope you realize how lucky you are. Better keep her hidden from the baron. He has an eye for beauty."

Stowig laughed. "Lord Geoff will keep his distance if he

wants peace in his family. That sister of his is too fond of their Norman blood to let him be familiar with a Saxon."

Matilda blushed hotly as Stowig turned to his wife. "William wants you to help his bride get acquainted in the village."

"Gladly. This time of day is pleasant for walking. Most villagers are still in the fields, but I can point out the best places for supplies." She grabbed Matilda's arm and dragged her outside to the roadway. "Let William rest here with Stowig while we get acquainted. After all," she winked, "a newly married man needs to keep up his strength."

Matilda looked about, interested. Some dwellings were old-fashioned earth houses with no windows, but many were wattle and daub. Matilda guessed most of them still had earthen floors. Most roofs were of straw and branches. After the rainy season, the cooking fires would be moved outside to reduce the chances of a dry roof catching alight. Windows often were covered with hide, but a few of the better-looking homes had shutters.

Pride rose at her cousin's husbandry.

Berwyn pointed out the homes of the elders who sat on the woten, the council of wise men.

"Caelfield is too small for its own town hall, so the woten meets at the manor. We did get a royal charter for a weekly market. That's unusual for a village this size. Our baron has clout at court because we hold a strategic position between the coasts."

"The manor also houses the visiting priest," Berwyn was saying, "and has a chapel to celebrate Mass. The baron is Catholic, but most of us cling to the old religion. Did you and William marry in the new or old religion?"

"The old practices," Matilda lied.

"How did you come to marry, if I'm not being too bold?"

A flush of guilt passed through Matilda as she prepared to deceive her new friend.

"It's a long story. The earl of my home village was forcing me into a betrothal with an abusive man. Cousin William rescued me by marrying me himself."

"I married young. And for love."

"William talks about his first wife."

Berwyn nodded. "Theirs was a great love. We thought he would die when Aelswitha did. He stopped eating and got gloomy for the longest while."

"I hope he doesn't think he made a poor bargain."

"Having met you, my dear, I'm sure he'll be content." Berwyn assured her. "And you as well. He's a decent man."

Matilda had already learned that.

She met women sitting by their cottage doorways making baskets from reeds that Berwyn said grew in the local pond. The meadows surrounding the village were covered with burdock plants, useful to make burrs for carding wool. The flocks had not yet been moved to summer pasture. As they strolled along the roadway, Matilda noted a tavern with rooms for wayfarers.

Berwyn slowed down and suggested they return. "That land at the end of the village only houses the cemetery," Berwyn was saying. "It'll take too much time to go that far. And you must be tired."

"I am." They turned around. "I'll visit the cemetery one day, though. William told me there's a striking piece of Anglo sculpture on a grave cover. I'm always interested in unique designs for my embroidery."

"You'll have to show me your work some day."

"I will."

Berwyn pointed up the hill. "You can see the baron's manor house from here if you look past those trees. Be careful. He makes young hearts flutter. Many a village woman falls in love, only to be disappointed."

Too late, she thought.

Chapter Eleven

The morning air was chilly when William rose to go to work. Matilda made sure he wore his hood that caped down over his shoulders. As the day warmed, he could remove this hood, but he would need it while the deep forest lay in the grip of this chill. His trousers were fastened around the waist by hemp, allowing the ample material to hang in loose folds for plenty of maneuvering room. Strips of leather confined the loose folds at his lower leg and doubled as straps to hold his smaller tools. She brought a mug of ale and a section of bread to break his fast and wrapped the remaining bread in a cloth for William to take with him. When he left, she started her chores, wanting to finish the hardest work of the day before the sun was high in the sky.

She fed the animals, grateful the barn had been thoroughly cleaned before their return from Wroxton, then put the cow and ox out to pasture and released the chickens. Now that the predators of the night were gone, the chickens could safely seek food outside their pen. Matilda freed the kitten, which stayed nearby as she worked.

After sweeping the cottage floor, she went to the cookhouse to put a stew on to simmer. Late morning, she decided to keep her hands busy by gardening. She was focusing all her frustration on the weeds—to their utter detriment—when she was startled by a nearby voice. She looked up.

"Dunavik. What are you doing here?"

"I bring news."

The chatelaine's bulk blocked the morning sun.

Matilda frowned and her stomach clenched.

"I'm not sure I want to see you. I mean no offense, but I'm trying to forget."

"Don't turn away from someone who's sympathetic. You may need an ear to listen to your worries."

The chatelaine sat on an overturned bucket near Matilda. She sighed as if relieved to be off her feet.

"There's a storm brewing at the manor," she said. "Lord Geoff's sister found out."

Matilda gave a strangled cry.

"Lady Rosamund is livid," Dunavik said. "She hates Saxons, but it's not the kind of thing the lady wants widely known. The baron just slams things and stomps off when his sister gets started. I tell you, it's a relief to get away."

She fanned her face with her hand.

Matilda dropped her gardening tool onto the upturned ground.

"I'm not sure I can bear this."

"What's done is done."

A voice hailed them from the roadway. Matilda looked up.

"Oh, I forgot about Berwyn. She's taking me to meet more of her friends. She'll wonder how I met you."

"I'll handle her."

They both rose. Matilda brushed herself off. Berwyn drew closer, a puzzled expression on her face.

"William's new bride tells me you'll be introducing her

around the village," Dunavik said. "I was thinking of doing that myself. We met yesterday when I came down to ask William to build some shelving. He wasn't here, but Matilda was. I came today to see how she's getting along. Now that you're here, I'll take my leave."

She said her farewells and trudged off.

"She's a good woman," Berwyn said as Dunavik disappeared into the tree-shaded lane. "She helps the sick and gives food and clothing to the poor. I suspect she stretches the baron's housekeeping monies doing this."

Dunavik had done her best to shield Matilda that first night and went out of her way to warn her today. Those were the actions of a good woman.

"At one time, we thought William might court her," Berwyn said, "but then we heard he was marrying you."

William's commitment to a sham marriage was a deeper sacrifice than her family had known.

By the time Berwyn finished talking about the village and its inhabitants, Matilda felt she knew Caelfield and its people very well indeed.

The women ate a midday meal and walked to the village. Matilda scrutinized each face they approached, worried that this would be the one who knew her secrets.

Matilda shifted uncomfortably in her chair that night and spun her empty food bowl in nervous revolutions. She and her cousin had just finished eating their evening meal after her return from the village. Agitated, she was acutely aware of raucous cricket sounds penetrating the room.

"William, have you heard any rumors about me?"

"No. Why?"

She dropped her hand onto the bowl to stop it from spinning.

"Dunavik was here today. She said the baron's sister found out. Sir Geoff fears our episode will become village gossip."

"I was the brunt of jokes about young brides, but nothing more. Her brother's involvement with a Saxon would be the last tidbit Lady Rosamund would want leaked in the village."

Matilda got up, collected her sewing basket and sat near the tallow candle to work embroidery stitches as she told of her day.

"I felt some women I met today were hostile."

William leaned forward in his chair.

"Who?"

"I can't remember names. One was tall, with brown hair, built on the thick side and a blemish on her right arm."

"Gwenver, wife of Oslad, the baker. She has reason to be wary of beautiful women. He strays."

"Oh."

"The other was probably Paela, her friend. Was she heavy, almost square of shape?"

"Yes, she was. I think I saw them gossiping about us yesterday as we started for home."

"More than likely, but it would be pure spitefulness. If they knew anything, they would've thrown it in our faces."

Chapter Twelve

With the dawn of each new day, Matilda tackled the chores. From milking the cow in the morning to washing up after the evening meal, she always found some task needing to be done.

"How did Mother do it? And with three children to care for, as well."

Occasionally, she went into Caelfield to barter for foodstuffs. Most of her time was spent alone, working from dawn to dusk. She and William wore the same exhausted look by nighttime.

A chore she particularly disliked was churning the cream into butter. Her shoulders and arms hurt long before that chore was done. She coaxed herself through the pain by reminding herself that butter made a soothing base for medicinal herbs to be applied to callused skin. By the increasing roughness of her hands, Matilda realized her mother's cream formulas of wool-wax and herbs couldn't keep pace with the ravages caused by everyday drudgery.

"At home, there were others to share the load."

Late morning, Matilda took a sturdy knife and a willow basket to forage for salad greens at the grassy edge of the roadway. There she knelt to cut tender dandelion shoots from the rich soil still moist from recent spring rains. The sky was clear and bright, the air full of the chirping of birds and the lowing of the cattle. The hum of a fat honeybee intent on extracting pollen from nearby clover added its tone to the contentment of the day.

"These dandelion will make a good spring tonic."

Matilda pushed her fingertips into the dirt, reveling in its soft moistness and the crisp feel of the young dandelion stalks. She placed the extracted plants into her basket and, not bothering to rise from her knees, moved to a new spot, to bend again to her task.

A curl fell forward, tickling her cheek. She pushed it back into place, leaving a smudge of dirt on her face.

In the distance Matilda could hear the lazy *clip-clop* of a horse. The sound stopped and the shadow of its rider fell across her. She twisted around to see who was there and her heart caught in her throat. The baron towered over her, his handsome countenance dark and stormy. Her momentary flash of happiness at seeing him after three long days of desertion vanished and a sense of danger took its place.

"What are you doing here?"

"This is my land. Everything on it belongs to me. Including you."

Love and hate—no never hate—warred within her. She rose from her knees, defiant.

"Go away."

Even with distance between them, she was aware of his sexuality reaching out. She willed herself to resist.

"I want you for my mistress."

Matilda's knees weakened. She gripped her knife tightly in her right hand. In her left one, she unknowingly squeezed the life from a newly harvested dandelion. She could have the man who captured her heart in her arms each night if she shamed herself. She gritted her teeth and straightened her back.

"You promised to leave us alone."

He straightened in the saddle, looming over her.

"You'll become old quickly with this kind of work," he observed. "I offer you rich clothes, fine foods and servants to do the work for you."

"Go away."

"You've become my obsession. I can't sleep for wanting you next to me."

The strain was evident on his features. He reminded Matilda of a hungry wolf.

"I'm married," she lied.

"That can be dissolved. You were a virgin."

Her heart beat erratically, seeming to want to tear itself from its anchorage. Her actions now would commit William and may very well get them both thrown off the estate, but she couldn't open her heart to Geoff only to have it break when he married a Norman lady. She had to resist. She couldn't give in.

"I want you," the baron insisted. "I can arrange it so you must submit."

"I'll kill myself first."

The words flew out of her mouth without her volition. She would run—as she had done before—but would never kill herself. She had too much respect for life and a deep belief that hers was meant to be a happy one. She must get away. Flee from temptation.

Geoff twisted as if readying to dismount. Matilda panicked and backed away, raising the knife to strike.

He settled into the saddle.

"I want to put the finest silks next to your skin, the most

delicately wrought jewelry around your neck."

Her senses relived the feel of the cerulean gown and scented bath water. She would experience luxury each day instead of these grinding chores.

"With me, you'll have music and art and love."

Geoff waved a hand

"Now, you have weeds and pigs and scouring."

Matilda's heart skipped a beat on "love". It was the only thing he offered that could tempt her.

The image of Sir Loric seaped into her mind and fear for her family rose.

"Leave me," she said. "You'd have me lose my self-respect. Get away from here. Go!"

But it was not Geoff who fled. It was Matilda who whirled about and raced for home, the digging knife clutched in her hand, her basket lying forgotten by the roadway.

"Wait," Geoff called after her, his voice holding entreaty. "Don't run from me. I won't hurt you."

"You've already hurt me," she flung over her shoulder. The pain of the dishonor put a stitch in her side as she ran. She grabbed at it as if by doing so she could somehow keep it contained.

On reaching the cottage, she threw herself onto the bed and soaked the bedding with tears of frustration until she escaped her troubles by slipping into a deep, exhausted sleep.

Geoff paced his richly furnished bedchamber in long, angry strides. He seemed eternally angry—at least each day since he'd set eyes on Matilda. The amount of discord she'd brought was not to be believed. He had probably condemned his soul to hell because of lustful thoughts. She affected him as no other woman before her. She drew him to her body and soul—despite all logical arguments.

He dropped into a wide-backed chair and laid his weary head upon the papers covering his sturdy, well crafted work table. He had done the unthinkable this morning. He'd cornered Matilda and hurled demands until she chose death.

Geoff pushed himself up and again paced, his riding boots loudly defining the level of his agitation.

"I should've known better."

He could be as persuasive as the next man—more so in most cases. Although he'd threatened, he wasn't the kind of man to take a woman by force. Impatience made him reckless. He could've slowly convinced her. Instead, he'd sealed his fate by having her fiercely repulse his advances.

He sprawled onto the bed on his back, his legs dangling to the polished floor, and allowed himself to feel miserable.

Matilda awoke to hear someone moving quietly in the cottage. She sat up on the bed, realizing she must look disheveled and flushed, but William didn't comment on it.

"I didn't mean to wake you," he said apologetically. "I decided to come home to eat."

He smelled of the sweat of honest toil.

"Are you all right?"

Her gut twisted into a knot.

"I'm fine," she lied, wondering if she would ever be fine again.

Now she had a third secret—one she must keep from William—Geoff's threat to take her as his mistress.

To escape such a threat they'd have to leave Caelfield. She couldn't bear to set in motion the measures that would tear

William away from everything important to him. She would wait and see if the baron would act or if he was convinced she'd never give in.

"Would you like something to eat?"

She shook her head, thankful for his kindness, wondering if he could see deception on her face.

"I'm not hungry, but I'll sit with you while you eat."

She rose from the rumpled bed and moved past her cousin to the table.

"What would you like?"

"I'll do it," said William. "You rest. You look exhausted."

She was about to protest, until she saw his need to care for her. She held back her words.

He moved back and forth from the cottage to the cooking shed and the root cellar, bringing utensils and foodstuffs to the table. Matilda contented herself with a mug of ale.

Usually a quiet man, this midday William made an effort as if to distract her by talking about Saturday's spring fair.

When it was time for him to return to work, Matilda slipped her arms around his neck and nestled her cheek next to his.

"Thank you, cousin, for being so understanding."

"I couldn't be otherwise."

As William disappeared from view, Matilda stiffened her resolve and set off to retrieve the basket of dandelions she'd left by the roadway. She was reluctant to return to the site of her confrontation with Geoff, but, as a practical matter, a part of their next meal lay there.

When she arrived, she grew distraught. Her heart plummeted to the pit of her stomach. Her hard work lay in ruins. The soft, woven basket had been crushed by the horse's hooves and the young dandelion plants lay in tatters. She rescued what she could, cupping the tender leaves in the folds of her skirt, but abandoned the damaged basket to the roadside ditch.

"My life mirrors the fate of these dandelions. Tattered and damaged."

Could it ever be repaired?

Chapter Thirteen

Matilda and William rose early Saturday to feed the animals and milk the cow before leaving for the spring fair on the market grounds. He offered to do most of the work to give her extra time to dress in festival clothes.

Seven days had passed since he'd found her on the bed— her pillow soaked with tears. She still jumped at every unusual sound, even though Geoff hadn't carried out his threat.

Because of the uneven ground at the fair, William insisted she wear her stout, mid-calf boots, the ones that laced up the sides and had thick soles. She wanted to wear something prettier. She laced the knee-length linen hose to eyelets in her under-tunic, dropped a multicolored tunic over her head and fastened it with her bronze brooch. She draped the veil of a *couvrechef* over her hair, fastening this headrail on each side with bone clips and tucking it into the neckband. Her cousin donned his blue tunic and brown leggings, which she had laid out on the chest, before putting on his three-quarter-length wool surcoat. Loose fitting and lacking sleeves, its front slits at elbow level allowed his arms to pass through. Matilda tossed the basin of dirty wash water onto the garden while William put on his boots.

"Ready?"

"Ready."

"Well, let's see what today brings."

As they headed toward the fair, Matilda was surprised at all the livestock being herded into town. Her curiosity pushed her anxiety out of her thoughts.

"There're a lot of sheep in Caelfield!"

"They're being brought in from winter pastures," William said. "The herders timed it so they would be here for the fair."

"There'll be more sheep than people."

"Hardly," William laughed, "but woolen goods are a large part of our foreign trade and a big draw at the fair."

"So I see."

"Caelfield's fair has been in existence so long it has prescriptive right. It doesn't need a royal charter, like fairs organized since the Normans. Charters are just the Crown's way of getting its hands on the revenues. Those sheep mean money for the herders, not the Crown."

Even before they reached the first cottages of the village, she could hear music and laughter. A couple exiting a nearby cottage called a greeting.

"I hear," the man said, "that the baron's sister is joining him today."

Matilda shook off the prickling fear attacking between her shoulder blades. Geoff and his sister would preside over the festivities, judge contests and sit at the head table for meals. She just needed to keep an eye out and stay away. She didn't expect Geoff to corner her in public, but she'd do all that was necessary to keep William from finding out about the threat to make her a mistress.

They drew closer to the market grounds and the roadway became more crowded. The variety of mingled sounds increased significantly. Domesticated dogs crisscrossed the roadway, seeming as excited as the humans to be going to a fair.

When they entered the main gate, Matilda's eyes opened wide. She'd never seen so much merry-making in one place. Flags waved gaily atop tents erected to house food, vendors, minstrels and fortunetellers. Several apprentices were at work cleaning vegetables under the large awning that would provide shade at mealtime. Animals were being bartered and others slaughtered for the midday and evening meals. Metal skewers of meat were rotating over dirt pit fires. The notes of a lute and the melodic alto of a singer drifted into and mixed in with the general uproar. Fascinated by the sound, Matilda stood on tiptoes. Although tall for a woman, she couldn't see over the many heads.

"William," she said tugging on his arm, "can you see where the minstrel is? I'd like to get close to hear what she's singing."

His great height carried him above the crowd.

"I can see her. I'll take you there."

They sat together on rugs laid end-to-end in the music tent. The minstrel was dressed in a gown using four differently patterned, colorful fabrics. She sang of heroic adventures. Most of the songs were in Anglo-Saxon poetic meter with head rhymes instead of end rhymes. Matilda was particularly fond of this style.

She held William's hand as they listened. They may be able to make something of their relationship—given time. Since true love was lost to her, companionship may be acceptable.

William is security itself, she thought. Geoff is the epitome of danger.

Poetry and music blended so poignantly that she was disappointed when the minstrel stopped. As they left, William placed a small coin in the bowl. Minstrels were willing to return to a hamlet where coins were plentiful.

They stopped to watch a competition on the green where men ran to a goal carrying heavy sacks of flour.

"Look. Carnulf is in the race!"

Matilda cheered for this young man who was apprenticed to William's friend, Stowig. Jumping up and down excitedly, she shouted encouragement. Carnulf came in third and waved to acknowledge that he'd heard her. She spotted Berwyn standing near the arena where a shepherd demonstrated the skill of his sheep dogs. William tugged her arm and urged her to go that way.

"It's Aelfred," he said, identifying the shepherd, "who cared for my animals when I went to Wroxton."

"He's really skilled," Berwyn pointed out. "See how he uses his hands to signal, as well as whistling?"

They watched the intelligent dogs work the sheep, cutting those marked with a black *X* out of the general herd and into a side pen. The dogs moved in a semi-crouch, ready to drop to their bellies and be still at a hand or voice command. This crouch calmed the sheep, keeping them from scattering before the dogs could move them into the side pen.

They said goodbye to Berwyn and bought a steaming meat and potato pie for their midday meal, taking the pie to the grass to sit and eat it. On a nearby lawn, a game of horseshoes had drawn a crowd. The ringing of each horseshoe as it clipped another and the thud as it hit the ground carried clearly.

"Are you enjoying yourself, William?" she asked as she rose and shook the crumbs off the cloth she'd brought for sitting on the ground.

"I enjoy watching you have fun."

Matilda took his arm as they walked. Several times, her

stout boots saved her ankles from turning over on the uneven fair grounds.

She paused to stare as a brightly clothed juggler tossed wooden blocks and a hunk of cheese into the air. Tippets, colorful pendant streamers, dangled from the elbow-length sleeves of his tunic. The tippets danced as he juggled. To the delight of the crowd, he started taking bites out of the cheese each time it landed in his hand. Everyone clapped and cheered him on. Matilda hoped he didn't have too many performances today or his belly would be feeling the worse with all that cheese. She became so absorbed she almost forgot to keep an eye out for Geoff.

They turned away and she and William wandered through the stalls, looking at the pottery, leather goods and the skillfully crafted gold and silver jewelry being sold.

"Hang onto your coins," her cousin advised. "The pickpockets like to work this section of a fair because of all the places to hide if spotted."

He'd have no trouble because he'd sewn a special pouch in his surcoat for his coins.

Her cousin purchased an iron knife blade to help her with the meals. Although she admired the ceramic Torksey ware, he seemed glad she wasn't tempted to buy because the price was high for his purse. There were examples of enameling and small quoit brooches, some in the style of belt-plate, as well as Frisian jewelry.

The smells of roasted meat and baked goods invaded her nostrils. They bought a small cake and sat down to eat.

"I have so much energy I plan to dance all night," she declared. "When I went shopping last week, several boys asked me for dances."

"I'm glad you have the village lads as dance partners. I'm

too old to dance all night."

Age was a wide gulf not easily conquered. Being young, she was looking for change and the excitement of discovering new things. Those fires no longer burned in William.

Choosing security has its price, she thought.

Some nearby villagers were describing a dancing bear act.

"Oh, a tamed bear. You have to take me," she begged.

"I've seen so many of those shows. There's only so much a trained bear can do."

"I can go on my own."

"Oh, no, you won't. I'll find someone to take you."

Carnulf, the blacksmith's apprentice who had run the sack race, stood nearby. He brightened and volunteered. "I'll take her."

William quickly agreed.

"I'll find Stowig and sit with him under the meal tent," her cousin said. "Meet me there afterward."

Matilda and Carnulf dashed toward the bear act.

Although she'd heard of such things, Matilda never thought to see a trained bear. The animal was huge and lumbered about. Its claws had been cut, its mouth muzzled and it had a stout chain restraining it.

"It must be expensive to hire such an act. How did it even get here?"

"Its handler has a cart made into a cage. They travel all over the country," Carnulf explained, edging them closer to the front of the crowd. "As to the cost, there's Lord Geoff. You can ask him."

He pointed across the road to the lawn set aside for competitions.

"No!"

Fortunately, Carnulf didn't seem to notice the distress his words caused. She ducked behind some people, but couldn't stop herself from stealing one glance. Geoff's back was to her and she saw him whisper into the ear of a beautiful woman whose arm was laced through his. The woman smiled and blushed.

An arrow of pain shot through Matilda's heart.

What is Matilda doing with that young buck? Geoff thought. How can she look so happy when I'm not? Where is William? She needs a taste of her own medicine.

He turned his back to bend and whisper an observation on the fair to his sister's friend. To his surprise, she blushed, probably because he'd been ignoring her up to that point. Well, she finally got his attention. And she would keep his attention. Hard though it was, he was training himself to stay away from Matilda.

Geoff turned his head just enough to see if his efforts were successful. He saw her stricken look before she hid behind some people.

He immediately regretted his impulsive act.

He claims to be totally smitten by me, Matilda thought angrily, and yet he's making that woman blush.

Vivid memories of their long night of love crept into her head. She resolutely pushed them out, but not before her body flushed in response.

Be careful, she warned herself. He'll have you responding to his signals the way those dogs responded to Aelfred.

She was about to suggest to Carnulf that they leave when

Geoff whispered once again in the woman's ear. At her nod, they both left the green and walked farther down the road. Relief and disappointment vied for ascendancy in Matilda's heart.

A roar from the bear scared her, bringing her back to the performance. Watching the act, she realized her cousin was right. The bear didn't have many tricks.

After checking in with William, she grabbed Carnulf's hand and dragged him away to the sack race, where they signed up as contestants. Geoff would be monitoring the archery contest, so there was no possibility of his coming up on them, no need for her to witness another woman's blush. With her leg and Carnulf's tied into a large flour sack, they raced for the finish line, falling several times, struggling to get up and then racing along as if crippled by a stiff leg. Although they didn't win, they ended at the finish gasping for breath and laughing at the spectacle they'd made.

Seated near the finish line was a beautiful woman in elegant attire and a jeweled cap of brocaded silk. She spoke loudly.

"These lower classes don't know how to maintain womanly dignity. That's why we Normans only associate with noble-born Saxons. At least they know how to conduct themselves."

"So true, Lady Rosamund," said her companion, a matronly Norman lady.

Frozen, Matilda stared directly at the first speaker to the point of rudeness. This was Geoff's sister.

Rosamund turned and stared at her. Matilda panicked. Her breath caught in her throat.

Not wanting to tangle with the lady, she cowardly decided on retreat and tugged Carnulf away.

They quickly returned the sack to the officials and agreed

to go to the tent of a fortuneteller. There, sheltered from the public eye, Matilda's heartbeat slowed and her breathing returned to normal.

The fortuneteller was dressed traditionally in many multi-colored skirts, with a shawl and kerchief. After crossing the seer's palm with William's coin, Carnulf was told that he would have many children around him. When it was Matilda's turn, the fortuneteller looked at her palm for some time. She traced patterns with her finger and wrinkled her brow.

"Why the frown?"

"I like to give a happy reading if I can, my dear," the fortuneteller said in somber tone, "but your future is looking stormy. You'll have to make a major decision shortly. Your choice will affect the rest of your life. May your choice be a wise one."

Matilda dismissed the foretelling as being too late. Geoff had already brought a storm into her life. She'd already decided to cut him from her heart.

"Ho, ho, ho," Carnulf laughed. "You're deciding to leave William and run away with me so I can have all those children."

"You think too highly of yourself. What reason would I have to leave William?"

He grinned teasingly.

"My strong arms and handsome face."

"William is my rock," she said. "He protects and takes care of me. I'll not leave him."

At that moment, she believed it implicitly.

A sing-along had begun in the meal tent when Matilda and Carnulf got there. William sat with Stowig and Berwyn. Her cousin made room on the bench. Matilda noted that the baron's table couldn't be seen. She and Carnulf sat down and joined in the singing. Soprano and alto, bass and tenor blended, with off-key voices filling in the gaps.

When evening meal hour arrived, food literally covered the tables. Matilda was amazed that a hamlet could have so much left after the winter season. She ate her fill and then some. Fully satiated, she sprawled on the bench—feeling as if she never wanted to move again. William left to talk with friends. Conversation swirled and eddied around her.

Later, musical instruments tuned up and the caller announced the formation of the first dance. A change came over the crowd as it tried to arouse itself. Matilda hadn't seen William for the last half hour, but she hoped he would come to her soon—she'd like her first dance to be with her cousin.

She'd just decided to hunt him down when he appeared and escorted her to the circle of couples forming on the dancing green. With precision, he led her through the patterns. As the music ended, he bowed.

"That's it for me. You'll have to accept the offers of these other lads. I'll be on the bench, talking with Stowig."

Matilda did just that. She danced and danced and only sat when she had no breath left. As soon as she could, she was up again. Her thoughts were totally on the music, her body responding to its beat. Her face felt warm and her breath came in short bursts. Her hair had long since escaped its covering and cascaded around her face. Worries were forgotten as she lost herself in the pleasure of the dance.

Night had long since fallen. Crackling bonfires sent wavering patterns of light across the darkened green. Crickets competed with the musicians and added their tones to the musical sounds.

Matilda turned from her last dancing partner to the one

standing behind who had put his hand on her waist. Immediately, she was whisked into the exuberant steps of a country dance, with not a moment to catch her breath. Strong hands led her into a twirl and it was only as she came out of it that she saw her dance companion.

Geoff!

She faltered, but was dragged along into the next pattern. Her feet automatically responded, which was just as well because her brain failed her. She couldn't protest. It would be unthinkable to cause a scene after dancing with most of the men in Caelfield this night.

She should be angry with him for his trap, but she could not be. She should be distant and cold, but with him those emotions were not in her repertoire. She longed to move closer than was proper, but somehow found the strength to resist.

Geoff said not a word, but, whenever his hand touched her to lead her into the next segment of the dance, he'd let it linger longer than necessary. Matilda knew she should pull away, but couldn't bring herself to forego his touch. She hated when the dance caused them to part and longed for the times when it brought them together. She should hate herself for wanting it so.

Conscience be damned. In the flickering light, she gave herself up to the joy of the dance. She breathed in Geoff's scent of soap and leather as if it were the food of life. She escaped into the trance evoked by his eyes. She drifted toward heaven with no care for the future.

She was glad that her feet followed the familiar dance steps on their own because she had no willpower to force them to act. Her body vibrated to his touch, evoking memories of their night together. She allowed the feelings to flood over her, creating a need in her loins that couldn't be satisfied. Her fate took on a dreamlike quality. She was transported from this dancing green to that bedchamber and to the awakening of her body that she still couldn't fully comprehend, but would forever cherish.

When the dance ended, Geoff bowed and disappeared into the crowd. To Matilda, he took joy itself with him.

The night sounds seemed muted, the dancers no longer as happy as they had been, the music embodying less vitality. She felt depleted and her body trembled.

Slowly, she walked alone off the dancing green—as if passing through a dream—to sit with William at the table. She pleaded exhaustion and declined other offers—not wanting to dilute the memory of that one miraculous dance.

Later, as she returned with William to their home, she realized that Caelfield no longer symbolized the secure and peaceful life she'd envisioned when she'd fled Wroxton.

The fortuneteller may have had the right of it.

Chapter Fourteen

Two days had passed since the fair. Matilda was shelling peas, breaking off an end and running her finger down the seam to release the firm, green peas into the bowl on the cottage table. She threw a pod into a basket and had just started on another when Geoff appeared in the doorway.

She rose from her chair. Her heart beat as rapidly as if she'd run two miles.

"Why are you here?"

A painful expression rippled across his face.

"I've been in torment since I left you sleeping in my bed."

He shook his head despairingly.

"I vowed to stay away. My determination slips as soon as I see you."

His mien was that of a supplicant. He advanced toward her.

Matilda backed across the room until her legs pressed against the sturdy bed whose wool curtain had been drawn to one side this morning.

"That's nothing to me," she lied. "You forced that night on me."

"I died inside watching you dance with other men. I had to dance with most of the women in Caelfield before I could hold you in my arms with propriety."

His anguish was palpable and hung in the air of the cottage.

"What do you expect of me?" she asked, with rising panic.

"Come live with me," he pleaded. "You can have anything you want. I'll risk discord in my family to have you by my side."

"Do you offer marriage?" Matilda asked, deliberately misconstruing his words.

"You know I can't."

"The first moment you lose interest," she said, indignation stiffening her backbone, "I'll be tossed away like those pods I just shelled."

He winced, but argued, "But as a rich woman. Independent. Wealthy."

"That has no value to me. I value my honor."

Her weakening legs started to tremble. Needing to take the strain off, she sank onto the edge of the bed.

Geoff paced the cottage floor, his body rigid with pent-up emotion.

"If you cannot give me your whole heart, just give me enough to assuage this hunger."

"Never."

The word allowed no misunderstanding.

"You value yourself too highly, Matilda. You are the daughter of a craftsman. You lack the social status to carry your beauty beyond the poverty of that birth."

Her mouth dropped open.

"And what about my self-respect? You'd leave me as a shell after stripping away everything I value!"

He strode angrily toward her, towering over her as he

closed in. Her heart speeded up. A shiver traveled down her spine as she leaned away.

"Settle for what you can get. I'm young, strong, rich. Take what life offers instead of turning it sour."

"If you were in William's place as a woodsman and I were your bride, I'd be happy, but honor doesn't allow me to be a man's mistress."

His body visibly shook with his rage.

"You toss my overtures in my face? And for what? Stupid pride."

Geoff grabbed her shoulders and shook her. His head descended and his lips claimed hers in a kiss that heated every surface of her skin. She struggled to break free.

"Release me before we're both destroyed."

When he released her, she fell across the bed.

"I broke a lot of rules for you."

"I cannot give you my love. William will always be between us."

Running his fingers through his sandy hair, he shook his head as though to clear it of some disturbing thoughts that needed the light of day. He cursed the fates who put her in his path. His voice sounded hollow when he said, "I acted against my principles to have you."

His expression showed how bitter this had been for him.

"I soon must marry to breed sons. When I wake each morning and find she is not you, what will become of me?"

His voice sounded flat with despair.

Matilda pulled the bed covering around her and held it tightly under her chin as if it could shield her from the cold chill of reality.

"I can be no man's mistress."

Geoff flung an oath and turned, his powerful legs taking him in long strides across the floor. He pushed the door violently as he passed, slamming it against the cottage wall with a crash like summer thunder.

The fortuneteller's prediction was coming true.

Her head ached and her shoulders seemed to carry the weight of the world. To save William, she may have to leave him in Caelfield and find some other place to live—a place where Geoff had no power over her.

She dragged her emotionally drained body out of the cottage and into the cooking shed to prepare soup for William's supper. She'd just finished chopping the vegetables and dropping them into the pot on the spit over the cooking fire when the kitten strolled by, looking completely in control of her domain. She rubbed against Matilda's leg and started mewing.

"Need some company, My Fate? Come. Let's discuss the state of the kingdom."

She stirred the soup one last time, then picked up the kitten and carried her to a chair under the apple tree. When she had the kitten settled in her lap, she inquired of her, "Why does love bring joy one moment and misery the next?"

The kitten gazed into Matilda's face and extended tiny claws to prick her leg as if to answer, "Pain is a part of life."

Matilda gently extracted the claws.

"Perhaps it's true what they say," she mused, trying to sort through her turbulent emotions. "Love is like the summer rain. One time it brings blessed relief to parched earth. The next time it brings floods and misery. Sometimes we fear the thunder's roar only to learn it's the spectacular lightning that's our enemy."

The kitten got up, circled several times, then settled itself contentedly onto her lap.

"You're right, My Fate. I shouldn't try to puzzle out the whys. I should make the best of things and find some way to be happy. I'll work this out."

She sat quietly, stroking the kitten, until it was again time to check the soup. Tonight, when she served supper to William she vowed to serve a confession as well. He deserved to know about the secret meetings and that she was being pressed to become Geoff's mistress.

Sunshine entered the cottage door when William returned from the market a short time later. His countenance was anything but sunny.

"I heard rumors," he said, his voice rigidly controlled, "rumors that you're making a fool of yourself with the baron."

Perspiration rose on her forehead. The secret had leaked before she could speak to William.

She raised her chin determinedly.

"He pursues me," she replied, her voice as calm as she could muster. "I rejected him twice. He met me one time by the road and, today, he came to the cottage. He wants me for his mistress."

William's back went extra rigid.

"And you didn't tell me? What were you thinking?"

His distress hung heavily in the air. Her heart abandoned her body, leaving a gaping hole of ache.

"I was going to tell you today."

He grabbed his head at his temples, his fingers disappearing into his hair as he gripped his scalp.

"I don't like being blindsided like this. His mistress! That's worse than the rumors. Nothing was said of his interest in you."

So it hadn't been revealed after all.

Matilda paced, the train of her kirtle sweeping the wooden floor. "What are they saying?"

"That you flirted with the baron at the dance and are pushing yourself on him. The words 'slut' and 'adulterer' were spoken."

"That's a lie! I'm innocent of this."

"I saw you dance. He approached you."

"My good name is being smeared."

Matilda shuddered, envisioning the scorn heaped on behind her back.

"I denied him. I thought that would end it."

"It didn't end it if he returned today."

William brought his hands down, clenched into fists.

"Deception is worse than learning an ugly truth."

"I'm sorry. I thought I was shielding you."

She nervously twisted the rough material of her work-stained kirtle.

"I'll leave Caelfield. I'll find some place to hide from him."

"That's not practical. Besides, I won't abandon you."

He slumped onto one of the chairs.

"Oh, William, I'm sorry you're hurt by this."

She knelt to put her arms around his waist and rest her head upon his lap. He combed his fingers through her freshly washed hair.

"What shall we do?" she asked.

"We must wait and see. Over the years that I worked for his

family, he's been an honorable man. I pray honor will conquer this madness."

"And the gossip?"

"If there truly is nothing going on, the talk will die out on its own."

"So we do nothing?"

"I want to continue living here. To be on the safe side, though, you should put together a traveling pack. Enough for a day's journey. I'll arrange for the animals' care and for someone to look after the cottage in case we must leave in a hurry."

"But my things…"

"We'll have to leave them. I'll barter for some horses to take us."

"Where will we go?"

"We'll go back to Wroxton and decide what to do from there."

Back into Loric's reach. Of the two, she'd chance the baron.

"A favor, William. Talk with Dunavik. See what she knows. We may be overreacting."

Matilda watched him, fearing he might want to avoid the manor house. His face registered determination to do the right thing.

"I'll go after I eat something. If we eat now, I'll have daylight for at least part of the journey."

Whether her chill was caused by the coming night or by an uncertain future, Matilda didn't know, but she draped a warm cape over her shoulders before hurrying to the cooking shed to bring their supper. The barnyard animals were settled for the night. The chickens were still out of the hen house, scratching at the dirt and uttering soft clucks. With a flutter of wings and squawks, they expressed annoyance at the disturbance she made as she passed on the way to the root cellar.

"I ruffled more feathers today than yours," Matilda commented wryly as she hurried by.

William left for the manor shortly afterward, taking his cloak and carrying a torch for the return journey.

Not wanting to dwell on her problems, Matilda kept busy. She filled a bucket with water to wash the dishes, using the last of it to make sure the cooking fire was well and truly out. She put the bowls and plates back onto their shelves and ran a wet rag over the wooden table. The nights were getting warmer, so she decided they didn't need a fire in the cottage, but, just in case, she laid kindling in the hearth in readiness. When the chickens returned to their roost, she latched the gate to keep the weasels out.

She heard William approaching and ran to him.

"Keridwen is spreading the rumors," he said. "Dunavik will try to learn more. She'll come to see us tomorrow."

Matilda's chin went up.

"This ruin of my good name must stop."

Chapter Fifteen

Dunavik arrived shortly after the breakfast hour the next day. Matilda was working in the garden, taking advantage of the morning coolness. William had already left for his labors in the forest.

Winded from the walk down the steep path, the chatelaine refused to say a word until she'd rested, declaring she'd return to the manor by the road, which was longer, but less steep. Once comfortably seated at the cottage table with a mug of ale and cheese at hand and with her feet up on a stool, Dunavik announced, "You're being crucified, my dear, and that Rosamund is behind it."

"Lady Rosamund?"

Matilda's breath caught in her throat.

Dunavik bobbed her grayed head.

"Yes, the baron's sister. She's evil, that one."

"I thought she wanted the whole thing hushed up."

"Oh, she keeps your night with the baron under wraps—she doesn't want anyone to know he has an interest in a Saxon. What she's doing now is blackening your name so he'll have nothing to do with you."

Dunavik expelled a noise of disgust.

"She bribed that cat, Keridwen, to do her dirty work. Money

talks loudly with that one and Lady Rosamund doesn't mind paying."

"What can be done?"

The walls of the cottage seemed to close in as she waited for the chatelaine's reply. Dunavik sipped her ale.

"You can't do anything about Lady Rosamund. She's protected as sister to the baron. Keridwen we can do something about. Everyone knows her slandering reputation. We can use that against her."

"How?" Matilda herself was at a loss.

"Well, I, for one, can tell everyone that she's unhappy because the baron doesn't fancy her."

Dunavik smiled.

"I'll also remind Keridwen that Lady Rosamund will be going home in a couple of months. The baron is here to stay, so she'd better not get on his bad side."

Tension drained out of Matilda.

"You're so good to do this for William and me."

"My child, you don't deserve to have your name smeared."

The chatelaine nodded in confirmation of her words.

"Paela and Gwenver love to tell tales. I'll work up a good one that they'll fight over to spread around."

Matilda's jaw dropped.

"But they're the ones spreading Keridwen's lies!"

"When you've lived here longer, you'll learn those two are as changeable as the wind. It'll surprise no one if they gossip about Keridwen instead of you."

The rumors had been fabricated. Her secrets were still hidden.

"Bless you, Dunavik. My good name is important to me."

When William returned home later that evening, he was in a good frame of mind.

"You'll never believe what's happening," he said as soon as he entered the door. "Keridwen is being accused of false tales."

Matilda told him of Dunavik's visit, bringing on a warm smile of approval.

"She has a good head on her shoulders."

They speculated on how the campaign to counteract the rumors would succeed.

"We should go to the marketplace tomorrow," he said, "so everyone can see there's no rancor between us."

"That would dampen the rumors."

They put their heads together as they ate supper and made plans for attending the morning market.

Chapter Sixteen

Light showers during the night made the roadway muddy. William gave her his arm to steady her since she was carrying the basket of extra eggs. Her wooden clogs were more prone to slip than his leather boots. Harnessed to William's back were two small stools he had made in his workshop in the barn. A woolen coif kept her head warm in the cool, moist aftermath of the rain.

Although they exchanged greetings with families heading to work in the fields, William didn't stop and talk. Instead he guided her directly to his friend's cottage.

"If anyone knows what's going on, it will be Berwyn," William had said. "She keeps her ear to the ground."

After they were invited in and seated at the table, Berwyn began talking in her usual, no-nonsense manner.

"You two are not going to believe this. Gossip had it that Matilda was casting eyes at the baron!" Berwyn shook her head as if in disbelief. "Amazingly, another rumor started that Keridwen is the one chasing after the baron and that she picked on you, as a newcomer, to explain her lack of success."

Berwyn gave a half-laugh as if at the vagaries of human nature.

"Actually, Matilda," she said, "if a rumor was to start, I would've thought it would be about you and our apprentice.

You spent a lot of time with him at the fair."

"All with William's blessing," Matilda hastened to say, dumbfounded that anyone would think she had an interest in Carnulf.

Berwyn looked satisfied.

"I wanted to sit with Stowig," William said. "Yet, I didn't want to spoil Matilda's first time at the fair. How do you think people are likely to react to us today?"

"Hard to say. Some people will believe anything. I heard others say that Matilda danced with almost every man in the village and only once with the baron. Those people will treat you as usual. Others might cold shoulder you."

William glanced out of the open door at the sky. The angle of the sun indicated that the morning was rapidly advancing. Matilda wasn't surprised when he rose and re-harnessed the stools to his back.

"We need to get on our way. We need to stake out a spot at the market."

The best places were taken, so they chose a spot out of the mainstream and near the dry goods stall where lengths of wool and linen in many variations of colors and patterns were sold. Local weavers were quite skilled in the preparation and coloring of wool, marketing some of their cloth through merchants in the capital city, which eventually was shipped to France.

Matilda decided to bring her embroidery to market. She already traded some of it for their weekly washing since she hated what the long soakings in water did to her hands. She willingly spent hours at needlework to buy the luxury of a laundress.

While William positioned their stools so their clothing

would stay out of the mud, she set out the basket of eggs. When done, they chatted with nearby merchants. A few hours and many people later, they had sold all their eggs and one of the stools. Paela had even stopped by, confiding to Matilda, "I should have guessed right away the rumor was false because I saw you at the fair with Carnulf."

William stepped in to quash any new speculations.

"With my blessing. The fair was new to Matilda. Because I tire of it shouldn't keep her from enjoying the booths and competitions—or the dancing."

William was bartering the remaining stool for some fodder when three women riding sidesaddle drew near on spirited horses. Their saddles and bridles with silver inlay were of the finest leather. Braided ribbons adorned the horses' tails. The colors matched the women's riding costumes, creating a vibrant effect on this muddy, gray day. Matilda's teeth clenched. Lady Rosamund was one of the women.

Riding too fast through the market grounds, they splashed mud as people scurried to clear the way. Matilda ducked her head, hoping Geoff's sister would pass her by, but she halted her gelding, forcing the other riders to a sudden stop.

After maneuvering her horse so that her back was to Matilda, she called to a dry goods merchant to bring her some cloth samples. She rubbed the fabric between her forefinger and thumb, then returned the goods to the merchant saying, "Such common cloth is suitable for those who live here, but not for those of us who attend court. Coarse women who aspire above their station might think these cloths splendid."

Everyone nearby stopped talking. Matilda's face burned.

Quite without thinking she turned to Paela—who was still standing beside her—and said loudly, "Do you not find there are those who create malicious rumor, no matter how unfounded? And there are others so proud they believe everyone must share their same high opinion?"

Paela, to whom any controversy was like a banquet, jumped into the spirit of this battle of wills.

"You're right. It's a wonder how some will jump onto gossip and sling it around as if there were truth in it. In the end the mud clings to those who sling it," Paela said, happily ignoring her own role in the local gossip mill.

Rosamund's face darkened as she turned in the saddle to glare at them. She swung her horse around and galloped off, scattering the villagers. Her friends looked at each other, shrugged and followed slowly after her.

"That's telling her," a woman shouted, "but you two have made an enemy today."

"She's probably right," William said reproachfully.

Matilda was still steaming.

"I couldn't help myself. The words just sprang out of my mouth."

"I can't stand her holier-than-thou attitude," Paela said, self-righteously.

"Thank you for standing by me."

Matilda was sincerely grateful.

"If you had said nothing, I'd have been hung out to dry by my careless words."

Paela patted her on the forearm.

"Think nothing of it, my dear. I enjoyed myself immensely."

She turned to leave, a delighted smile on her face.

"I'm going to find Gwenver. She'll be sorry she didn't come to market today."

Matilda picked up her empty egg basket. As she and

William left the market, they mended fences and hoped they squashed any further speculation. Gossip about Lady Rosamund's slur was already circulating. Most chuckled at the sister's discomfort, but some voiced ominous warnings.

"She doesn't take humiliation lightly. Watch your back, Matilda, or you may find a knife in it."

Chapter Seventeen

That evening Dunavik unexpectedly arrived at the cottage.

"Lord Geoff wants to meet with you two here tomorrow," she said, panting, slightly out of breath. "He heard about the disturbance at the market today."

Matilda saw William grip the back of a wooden chair so hard his knuckles turned white. Her breath caught in her throat.

"We already took care of that," he said.

"Not very intelligently." Dunavik settled herself with a sigh into a chair. "Lady Rosamund is tearing about the manor in a rage. The baron wants to stand between you and his sister. He'll be here in the morning."

"Not with Matilda in the room," William said adamantly. "I'll talk with him alone."

"I'll try to persuade him to talk just with you. Let Matilda stay out of sight, but near enough if he insists on seeing you both. He gets the last word."

That night Matilda couldn't sleep.

In the morning, Matilda watched Geoff step silently onto the grass as she stood hidden by the cottage door. Her heartbeat increased despite her admonitions to herself to stay calm.

The baron had walked from the manor house, taking the path that hid him from prying eyes. One moment he wasn't there and the next he was. She marveled at the stealth with which he moved. He probably learned it during warfare training. Or perhaps it was natural.

William—expecting Geoff to arrive by horse—was watching the road.

Clothed in his best, her cousin wore a blue tunic and brown leggings ending in slipper boots that he usually only wore indoors. Matilda surmised he'd dressed carefully so as not to appear at a disadvantage. She'd dressed in her oldest and dullest clothing and put a kerchief on her head like the peasants wore. If she had to meet the baron today, she would look her worst.

William had taken the two chairs outside and put them under the apple tree, not too close to the cottage, but at an angle where Matilda could see without being seen. He was standing by them, watching the road. Geoff was almost upon her cousin, who still hadn't heard him. Matilda yearned to warn William, but if she called out she would attract Geoff's attention. She forced herself to wait.

"Good morning," the baron said as he drew near, his voice modulated to a conversational tone. The collar of his shirt of fine linen opened at the neck, revealing a gold chain and coin pendant worn nestled against his skin.

Startled, William spun around. He quickly regained his composure and replied in a cordial, but non-deferential manner.

"Good morning, my lord."

He gestured toward the chairs.

"Please be seated and rest yourself."

Geoff sat and began to talk even before her cousin had seated himself. To Matilda, this was an indication of his disquiet.

"My sister made slurring remarks yesterday. She shouldn't have discredited our local wool industry. Nor implied that your wife is a social climber."

William nodded, but said nothing. Matilda, on the other hand, flushed, flabbergasted that a baron would make such an admission. She'd been expecting Geoff to demand a humbling apology. Matilda allowed herself a relieved sigh that her hasty words didn't get her cousin into trouble. As she watched, a frown creased Geoff's brow. He leaned forward and continued in a determined voice.

"Lady Rosamund wants me to chastise everyone who laughed at her. Instead, I'm going to honor those she slurred. My sister needs a lesson in humility."

He tilted back in the chair as if his idea needed some distance to play itself out.

"Our parents spoiled my sister and allowed her snobbery to grow. I can't understand why. They themselves lived in harmony with you Saxons."

He shook his head, looking bewildered.

"She thinks she's better than everyone around her, including the women she brought as companions. Her husband, Maximilian, is even worse."

Matilda never could've imagined a baron talking this way to a retainer.

"My sister will learn that meddling will only get her the opposite of what she wants. I'm inviting you, the weaver's guild, and the Council of Elders, along with your wives, to a banquet at the manor. She must act as my hostess. Let her see all of you sitting at table with her."

The baron sounded as unbending as iron.

Matilda felt faint. She didn't want to go into the manor again. She lowered herself onto a nearby stool and fanned her face with her hand.

"This may not be wise, my lord." William's voice quavered, but his manner said he'd hold his own. As he spoke, his body took a more aggressive stance. Nearby chickens, scratching for food, seemed to sense the change.

"I don't want Matilda hurt. We should stay away from the manor."

Geoff tensed.

"It would look as if the rumors are true if you and your wife are excluded."

William appeared to stand taller to withstand this assault. Although proud to have her cousin champion her, an anxious shiver ran down her spine. Even freemen disappeared into dungeons.

"I'll not have her go into the manor and never come back. She'll be destroyed if she becomes your mistress."

Geoff first looked stunned.

"You know?"

"She told me."

"I'm surprised. Did she tell you she turned me down flatly?"

"She did."

Geoff ran fingers through his hair in agitation.

"I give my word. Matilda will leave the manor with you. She said, if I try to force her, she would kill herself."

This time, William looked stunned.

"She didn't tell me this!"

He sat back down as if his legs buckled under him and

glanced her way.

"She's impulsive enough to try," Geoff said.

From her stool behind the door, Matilda couldn't believe what she'd heard. She hadn't been serious about killing herself. She planned to run away. She'd made the threat in defiance. Strangely, those carelessly flung words were now her protection.

As Geoff rose to take his leave, he spoke in a quiet tone that brooked no opposition. "I'm holding the banquet this Saturday. You both must be there."

Once Geoff was out of sight on the road to the village proper, Matilda ran to her cousin to sit with him in one of the chairs under the shade of the apple tree. William emanated a calm maturity Matilda had come to rely upon. She owed him much and had given him little but controversy.

A pounding ache began in her head.

"Because of me, you're embroiled in a confrontation with your baron."

"It wasn't your doing, Matilda. You shouldn't feel guilt."

He patted her hand.

"It's nearly time for the midday meal. Suppose I bring food out here under the tree? Then we can talk."

William had spent the many years after his wife died taking care of himself and had added her to the care. She nodded gratefully and he left for the cooking shed.

The cow, turned out into the pasture with the ox, absently chewed a cud. Bees buzzed lazily among mock orange blossoms, which filled the air with cloying fragrance. All nature seemed at peace—with only her and William having their peace destroyed. They were caught up in a maelstrom.

In honesty, Matilda wasn't altogether unhappy about this

maelstrom. That force had brought Geoff into her life. At times she fervently wished she'd never seen Caelfield. Other times, she'd asked herself, "Was the passion of one night worth this unrest?" Often her answer was "yes".

Thus, the dilemma. Matilda felt torn.

William's presence brought a serenity she treasured. She bathed in its calming influence. She fed on its constancy.

Geoff on the other hand embodied her dream.

Ultimately, which was more important to her wellbeing— the compassion of William or the passion of Geoff?

She had no answer. She'd chosen to be ruled by her head and not her heart—but was this right in the long run?

William returned carrying a basket filled with nuts, bread and cheese. A jug of fresh water was crooked over his finger. While eating, they discussed the upcoming banquet.

"The baron is wrong on this," her cousin said.

"He's pig-headed. He'll never back down. We'll have to keep well away from his sister."

William nodded.

"I could be sick that night," Matilda speculated.

"If anyone discovered you weren't really ill, it would look like cowardice or guilt. Besides, the baron was adamant."

They speculated along these lines, considering their options one by one when Berwyn unexpectedly arrived.

"Isn't it wonderful?" She glowed with excitement. "Everyone is thrilled about the banquet. What are you wearing, Matilda?"

"Neither one of us thinks it's a good idea. We're concerned Lady Rosamund will find some way to ruin the evening."

"She wouldn't go against her brother."

"I hope you're right," William said. "With her, you never

know."

William offered Berwyn his seat before saying, "I'd better get some work done today."

He tied the sleeves of his tunic up above his elbows to keep his forearms free, revealing the muscles he had built up over the years. As he gathered his tools, he asked, "Would you and Stowig want a ride to the manor in our cart Saturday?"

"Our"—yet another sign that William now shared his life with her.

Berwyn smiled.

"Absolutely. That way I can wear my best slippers and not get them dirty."

He left for his workshop in the barn to finish the wooden shelving for Dunavik. Although it started as a ruse to explain Dunavik's having met Matilda, the ruse had turned into reality and would give William income.

Matilda spent the next half hour with Berwyn matching clothing and jewelry to decide what she should wear to the banquet. Her heart wasn't in it. If she had her druthers, she'd look her worst—but the villagers would take that as an insult to their baron. Letting Berwyn have her way seemed easier.

Chapter Eighteen

Two nights later, Matilda reluctantly followed William to the cart to travel to the manor. Her harvest green kirtle—chosen by Berwyn during her visit—was made of lightly woven wool. She herself had tatted the green netting holding her hair in place. Her mother had made the ecru lace trim of her kirtle. A cloak of scarlet—like trees in autumn—covered her shoulders, held in place by the ornate bronze clasp. Her dyed green leather slippers were a gift from her cousin.

William had offered rides to two elders and their wives. Along with Berwyn and Stowig, they filled the cart to overflowing, but it had the advantage of legitimizing the party of travelers. No villager would be rude after seeing her arrive with the wise men of the woten.

"She's beautiful like Aelswitha," the elder who was a goldsmith said. The unfortunate first remark set Matilda's heart pounding.

"No, not like Aelswitha," William replied. "Aelswitha had a fragile beauty. Her features were as delicate as the pottery she loved."

His eyes were alight with happy memories.

Matilda slid into the background, hoping no one would ask her opinion.

"I have to admit," the goldsmith said, turning back to

Matilda, "you don't have that delicate look. You look healthy and full of life, with perhaps a streak of mischievousness—or is that independence?" He laughed. "Now that I think about it, the only likeness between you both is that of beauty."

Matilda blushed. She was thankful when the other elder diverted the conversation by commenting unfavorably on Lady Rosamund.

"Her kind think they're better than us, but our ancestry is older. If the Conqueror had stayed home, we Saxons would be the lords and the Normans a bunch of foreigners come to trade."

Matilda tuned out the chatter as memories flooded in of her first glimpse of the manor house.

Its beauty in the light of the moon had been ethereal, and she had been so stunned by it, she'd stopped dead in her tracks. Tendrils of ghostly ground fog had beckoned her, inexorably drawing her ever closer to its imprisoning rear portal. Today, she was arriving in brilliant sunshine to the front door and surrounded by influential villagers.

As soon as the cart halted, a stable boy hurried forward to hold the ox's halter until all the passengers were safely aground. Then, he led the ox to the barn to unharness it and feed it.

Berwyn chatted with William as they walked toward the door. Matilda was unable to focus on their words. Laurels bordering the walkway emitted a delicate aroma, evoking thoughts of that other time. Turbulent memories coursed through her of she and Geoff unclothed on the bed in the master bedchamber.

The impressive door opened as they approached. A retainer—dressed in the baron's colors of green and brown—bid them welcome. He ushered them into a small cloakroom near the entrance. It bespoke wealth and taste. Matilda hung her cloak.

A porter directed them down a hallway to the main dining hall. It was paneled with Saxon strip decoration all the way to the top of the wall, where it met a carved ceiling. The floor was laid with Roman tile. Her feet exhibited the same reluctance to move across the tile as they did when she'd entered the rear portal. Her heart and her head were pounding.

Upon entering the dining hall, Matilda faltered, flushed slightly and grabbed William's arm. Geoff stood near the banquet table, greeting his guests. He looked magnificent clothed in a blue tunic with leather trim. She was chagrined to discover her eyes lingering and tore her gaze away.

"We need to move along," her cousin said.

She was grateful for William's supporting arm and tried to fade into the background.

Geoff ached with the first sight of Matilda. He watched her gaze roam the rectangular banquet hall, the largest chamber in the manor. Built as a communal room, it had no rooms above it. Its many tall windows were narrower than a person's body to guard against attack. During the day their shutters were thrown open to the meadow breezes, letting in the sounds of an active estate. The wide pavement stones were swept daily and strewn with herbs and straw to mask odors. Trophies of war and of the hunt, boldly colored banners and vibrant tapestries adorned the walls. Her gaze rested anywhere in the hall, but on him.

Enormous fireplaces, large enough to roast an ox, anchored either end of this chamber. Fires burned in both, though they were used for heat and light these days, not cooking. Candles were set into wall and table sconces.

Lady Rosamund and her guests arrived and were seated in a place of honor at an elegantly carved table, which formed a *T* to a series of oak tables down the center of the hall. His sister and the women wore the finest of materials, presenting the illusion of a royal assemblage. In dress, Rosamund outshone all. In looks, ugliness overshadowed her beauty as barely controlled anger contorted her refined features.

A footman announced the order of seating according to status in the village or on the estates. Sadness washed through Geoff as Matilda walked quickly to the far side of the hall, as if grateful to escape his presence. He sat down, determined to keep himself occupied so he wouldn't think of her.

"Serve the food."

Soon mouthwatering aromas pervaded the hall as stewards brought platters of savory meats to the banquet tables. Smoked ham, baked fish, roasted goose and stewed rabbit were followed by bowls of piping hot vegetables and breads still steaming from the oven. Sounds of feasting dominated as his guests settled in to enjoy themselves.

"Dunavik has outdone herself," he told his guests.

Lady Rosamund, eating stonily, looked as if she wanted to bolt from the chamber.

One time, Geoff looked up just as Matilda glanced his way. Impulsively, he winked. She flushed and regrettably didn't look toward him for the reminder of the evening.

"It couldn't have gone better," William said when they returned home that evening.

They were preparing to retire for the night. The ox had been unharnessed and put in the pasture. The cart would remain in the yard until daylight, when they'd move it into the barn. Matilda had carefully checked their best clothing for food spots and hung it up to air. Tomorrow, she'd fold the finery and put it away in the large chest. William had drawn a basin of water, and they were sharing it to wash up. She was grateful for the chores to do before retiring. They kept her mind occupied, as well as her fingers.

"The baron kept his promise;" she said, relieved.

"He kept Lady Rosamund in line. I believe the rumors will die down now."

"I hope so."

Her headache had disappeared once she realized neither the baron nor his sister would make a scene. When Geoff kept his distance, she knew it boded well for their continuing to live in Caelfield.

"The food was excellent," William was saying. "I wish we could afford such spices."

"It seems the baron can afford the best of everything."

Matilda wondered if Geoff planned that show of wealth to entice her to become his mistress. It was not enough to make her yield.

"What do you think tonight means for our future here?"

William thought for a while.

"We're better off than we were a couple of days ago."

"Inviting the elders to join us was an excellent idea."

"It protects us from the villagers, but Lady Rosamund is still a threat. Perhaps if you stay out of her sight, she'll forget about you. She'll soon return to her husband."

Matilda doubted it.

"Life is tough, Voernulf."

"Agreed, my lord."

The baron was walking beside his overseer Monday morning to a field where an irrigation ditch was being repaired. Warring emotions rampaged in his mind and heart.

"I'm overlord. You'd think I could get anything I wanted. But to do that I must hold a woman by force—which I won't do."

"You're talking about William's wife, my lord?"

Geoff's insides churned acid.

"I am—as you correctly point out—talking about the wife of William."

The conversation stopped while the men climbed the steps of a wooden stile that kept the animals out of the field. It was built to allow them to pass easily over the fence. As he climbed the small steps, Geoff noticed that the rows of vegetables near the fence were already ankle high.

The ground became spongier as they crossed the field nearest the creek that fed the irrigation ditches. They walked in silence for a while, their shoes picking up moist clumps of mud as they moved along.

"I don't understand her. She'll grub in the dirt and wear rough clothes rather than accept wealth as my mistress."

"Perhaps she's playing for higher stakes."

Geoff was jolted by the thought.

"She's a woman I find hard to stop thinking about."

"The liaison is unwise."

"At the banquet, I barely managed to stay away from her."

He looked sidewise at Voernulf.

"I know I must."

"You run the risk of getting the whole village up in arms if you don't."

Chapter Nineteen

Matilda and her cousin passed the blacksmith shop Tuesday morning on their way to the market. William carried a wooden stool and a couple of stout walking sticks. She carried her embroidery. Suddenly, a harsh cry rang out behind them and above a clatter of pounding hooves.

"Temptress. Harlot. You dare deceive me? And with a laborer?"

Matilda's knees grew weak. Her world crumbled around her.

"Sir Loric!"

The knight charged down the road on a lathered horse, his maille tunic of interlocking metal plates glinting threateningly in the sunlight.

"He's trying to run us down," William yelled as the horse closed in. He threw his three-legged stool. It bounced off the knight's shoulder, but it didn't topple him out of the saddle.

A roar of rage spread like evil through the air of the village, awful in the depth of its hatred.

"Attack me would you, peasant? You'll regret that."

Matilda ran into Stowig's shop to crouch behind a storage bin. She saw her cousin turn in the opposite direction, as if to confuse Sir Loric about her whereabouts. Her heart beat so rapidly it threatened to rip itself out of her bodice. Sheer panic nearly paralyzed her. She was finding it hard to breathe.

William stood on the roadway, legs braced. Two of his stoutest walking sticks were brandished as weapons in his hands. He wove them back and forth in front of himself to spook the huge horse and to protect against the morningstar's spiked metal ball. Matilda's breath caught in her throat as her cousin risked his life to protect her.

"Leave him alone," she screamed from her hiding place. "It's me you want."

"You'll get yours when I finish with this cur."

One of her cousin's walking sticks bounced onto the roadway when the whirling morningstar wrapped its chain around the wooden shaft, ripping it from his hand.

"William, here," Stowig shouted.

She saw her cousin turn in time to catch the long, iron bar Stowig had thrown. He faced the knight once again.

The morningstar whirled. It clanged against the iron bar, but unwrapped itself before the bar could be yanked from William's hand. Although her cousin stumbled forward, he quickly corrected his balance and stayed on his feet. Villagers were running up the roadway toward them.

The knight circled his winded horse for another charge. Before he could get into position, the baron galloped up, halting his massive warhorse directly across Loric's path. A blinding pressure made her head ache as Geoff put himself in danger with no more protection than a linen tunic.

"Who fights my retainer?" he roared.

"Loric, Knight to the Earl of Wroxton."

"What cause?"

"Matilda was promised to me. She sneaked off—and with a

woodcutter," Loric bellowed, a fierce scowl marring his face.

"All who live in Caelfield are under my protection," Geoff bellowed back.

"I will extract my justice."

"Leave or forfeit your life."

"Not until I kill this upstart and drag that harlot down the road by her hair."

"You just signed your death warrant."

The baron drew his dagger from the scabbard attached to his saddle with his left hand and thrust out his right hand to William.

"Your weapon."

Her cousin placed the iron bar securely into Geoff's hand before retreating into Stowig's shop. Matilda held William tightly as they sheltered behind the storage bin.

"So be it," Loric cried out, then charged.

Geoff held fast to the bar, using it like a lance while urging his horse forward. Clouds of dust obscured the horses' hooves, but their pounding intensity reverberated in Matilda's ears. She heard an "oof" from Loric as the iron bar rammed into his side, causing him to mis-aim the morningstar.

Both steeds spun around.

They charged.

Geoff turned aside, but not far enough. The spikes of the morningstar danced over the shoulder of his linen tunic, drawing blood. He winced from the pain of those punctures. Matilda echoed the pain.

On the third pass, Geoff unseated Loric. Jumping from his horse, he ran toward the knight, who was scrambling to his feet. Each threw aside the cumbersome weapons in favor of daggers for close fighting. Matilda saw a villager sneak in to steal away and hide the morningstar.

The clang of metal blades seemed to go on forever, instead of the few minutes it took before Geoff tripped Loric and leapt on top of him.

"Repent your false words."

"Never."

The knight raised his dagger two-handed over his head to plunge it into Geoff's back. Before he could, the baron drove his dagger deep into Loric's throat. He pushed up from his knees and stepped away as the knight's lifeblood stained the roadway.

Geoff is alive, Matilda rejoiced. I'm saved from Sir Loric!

The man she loved was walking away from the fight and the reason behind the pretend marriage lay dead in the roadway.

Matilda's knees weakened. She wrapped her arms around William's waist when he bent down and lifted her to her feet. She lay her cheek against his chest and drew strength from her cousin, even as she hardened her heart to keep from rushing to Geoff.

"Are you all right?"

"No injuries."

William had stood his ground. A fight by a woodcutter against a mounted knight must take a toll—even if there were no physical wounds.

She stepped away as villagers flocked around her cousin, slapping him on the back and congratulating him for standing up to a knight. They cheered and clapped, causing a black bird, recently settled in a nearby elm, to fly off in noisy protest.

Invitations to celebrate at the tavern came. Her cousin looked flushed and embarrassed from the attention.

"Go with your friends. I'll see to the baron's wounds and

then I'll meet you there."

Matilda steeled herself to remain outwardly calm as she crossed the packed dirt to Geoff. She averted her eyes from the sprawled remains—grateful it could no longer rise up against her. Several people were heading back to the market grounds. Dogs criss-crossed the bloody roadway where Geoff was instructing some men to remove the body and prepare it for transport back to Wroxton. Sir Loric's page was among them. He looked surprised—but not unhappy—that his master was dead.

She called out to Geoff, her heart in her throat.

"Let me look at those wounds, my lord. I'm skilled in healing."

He looked up and her heart leapt.

"I can get these attended at the manor."

"Better not get more sweat and dirt into those cuts. Sir Loric may have primed his weapons with excrement before he fought. Such wounds fester quickly."

She signaled to Carnulf who was walking toward them.

"Hurry to my cottage for my Simple Chest and a basin, Carnulf. Bring a jug of spring water from the barrel by my cookhouse."

"I am a slave for a beautiful woman," Carnulf said as he bowed before racing toward her cottage,

Matilda pointed to a bench outside the blacksmith shop.

"Sit down, my lord, so I can tend to you."

Geoff crossed the roadway with her and sat. He seemed exhausted.

"Are you in pain?"

"Not much."

"This tunic must come off so I can get at the wounds."

She grasped the bottom to pull it over his head, shivering from the memory of the last time his chest was bared to her. Heat and sweat and exhaustion poured out of him.

Geoff gingerly worked his arms out of the sleeves. A few times his arm brushed her body. Where it touched inflamed her with desire as if their bodies recognized each other and could not resist a response.

Matilda folded the tunic and set it on a nearby storage bin. Her fingers tingled as she pressed one of the embroidered handkerchiefs intended for sale at market against the abrasions, soaking up the rivulets of blood so she could examine the wounds.

"None require stitches. If we can keep them from festering, you'll heal in no time."

She imagined taking care of him every day, but that could only happen as a mistress. Possessing neither wealth nor position—even though freed from Loric—marriage was out of the question.

Carnulf arrived with the Simple Chest. He poured water into the basin while she removed a powder which induced healing. With an unsteady hand, she shook some into the tepid water.

She dipped the handkerchief and started cleansing. Tears threatened at the touch of skin torn by the metal points of the morningstar. When finished cleaning the wounds, she brought out a quantity of salve base and put it onto a metal plate she had removed from her chest.

"I'll use an herbal salve to reduce the chance of scarring."

Geoff sat quietly under her ministrations.

With a tiny metal spoon, she extracted ground herbal powder from each of three opened containers. She cleansed the spoon with water each time, drying it on a linen square so that one powder wouldn't contaminate another in the containers before mixing them into the salve base. She used a metal knife to lift a small quantity of salve and press it to each cut.

As she worked, she quietly sang the healing songs. Geoff was Catholic and wouldn't understand Saxon healing practices, but she wanted to take no chances. It was another reminder of their cultural gulf. Her alto tones seemed to be a calming influence to the Saxon villagers looking on.

She placed clean, gauzy cheesecloth over the wounds, telling Geoff to hold it in place. She smoothed wide strips of bandaging over his muscled shoulder, relinquishing her precious supply without a qualm. She was content to give something of hers to Geoff.

Only after every injured spot was covered did she stretch the ends and tuck them under the bandage. She rose from the bench.

"Rest today," she said in her most controlled voice. "Keep this clean. You should be healed in a few days."

"My grateful thanks."

She nodded and repacked her chest. Her excuse to be close to her lover was at an end, but she knew what was required of her. She headed for the tavern and William—leaving Geoff sitting there.

Chapter Twenty

Early in the morning two weeks after the death of Sir Loric, Matilda carried the special knife she used for mushrooming and a medium-sized basket into the forest. For almost an hour, she dug mushrooms out of the soft soil, moving deeper into the forest as she searched for them.

She kept a sharp eye out because sometimes a flint arrowhead or a stone tool crafted by the ancients could be found. Her parents had come across several near their Wroxton home.

Matilda heard a sound. She cocked her head and concentrated, recognizing the tones of a recorder—a wooden flutelike instrument with eight finger holes. The melody seemed filled with sadness and longing.

Without thought, she sought out the player of this sorrowful tune.

Dense treetop foliage cast deep shadows even at high noon. Matilda's passage toward the musician was unhindered by small brush and her footsteps muffled by damp, thick layers of fallen leaves.

Familiar with these woods from other mushrooming excursions, she knew she was approaching a clearing. Growth began to take hold. Dogwood encircled the clearing and took advantage of small patches of sunlight to bring forth blooms.

Hiding behind foliage, Matilda listened to the plaintive melody. Curiosity got the better of her—despite the danger from encountering a stranger while alone in the woods. Stealthily, she pushed aside the branches.

"Geoff!"

He rose, looking perplexed, but pleased.

"Matilda! What are you doing here?"

"Hunting mushrooms. I followed the melody, expecting to find a traveling minstrel."

"I'm glad you did."

Geoff patted the boulder on which he'd been sitting.

"Come sit with me."

Matilda shook her head. The rock was large enough, but it would put her too close.

"I'll step into the clearing for a while," she heard herself saying, even while her inner voice screamed that it wasn't a good idea, "but I can't stay."

As she pushed her way through the branches and set her basket on the ground, she felt no urgency to retreat. Geoff seemed easier to be close to today—more mild than his usual intense self. She pulled a cloth from her pocket and wiped dirt from her hands as she looked at him.

Sturdy leather gloves like those used for hawking were lying on the boulder. Beneath Geoff's ankle-length tunic, his loose trousers were tied at the bottom by leather cords. His feet were encased in old-fashioned shoes made of a single piece of rawhide with fur inside. Over these he wore pattens, a wooden overshoe. His hair was free of covering, unlike Matilda's, which was covered with a kerchief like those the farm women wore to keep debris out while digging in the earth.

A squirrel stopped and looked at them. Sitting on its

haunches, tail curled high and front paws raised, it sniffed the air. After a moment, it moved on as if realizing these two were intent on each other and would not be throwing tidbits its way.

"This is a wish come true," Geoff confessed.

A warm flush spread throughout Matilda.

"As you treated my wounds, I wanted to throw you on the ground and make love to you."

She laughed.

"I'm glad you did nothing so foolish. How are your wounds?"

He rotated his injured shoulder and shook his arm loose.

"Good. Almost back to normal."

Geoff sat, patting the boulder invitingly.

"Are you sure you won't join me?"

Once again she shook her head.

"I don't want rumors to start up. Probably no one will come this far into the woods, but I can't take chances."

Geoff wrinkled his brow.

"Why was that knight attacking you and William?"

A large lump stuck in her throat. She must choose her words carefully. The pretend marriage still protected her honor.

"I left Wroxton before its earl forced me into marriage with him. He was a vicious man. He tracked me down and would have killed us both if you hadn't fought him."

"I was on my way to the market in hopes of seeing you."

"We were heading that way."

"It took me a bit to figure out that William was fighting a knight."

"My cousin is a brave man."

She bit her lower lip. She should have said husband.

"Sir Loric is out of your life. He can't harm you."

And Loric took with him her reason for staying in Caelfield. She should release William from his family duty and return home. She should, but couldn't. Not yet.

"Will the earl take revenge on your family when Sir Loric's body is returned?"

"I don't think so. His late wife was cousin to my mother. In fact, he just stood in for our late father for a family wedding. It's the one good thing to come out of this."

"Whose?"

"Sir Loric's page told me my sister was married last week."

Geoff leaned back, smiling engagingly.

"Romance is in the air."

Matilda's heart beat wildly. How could she be a woman and not respond to such a man?

Truth be told, she was glad to be alone with him. In the end she must walk away, but to indulge herself for a short time surely couldn't be so terrible.

"I didn't know you played a musical instrument," he heard her say, breaking him out of mental clouds.

"There are many sides of me you don't know," he replied, regretting there would be no opportunities.

"The tune was sad."

"Without you, I can't be happy."

Superstitiously, she knocked on wood to ward off any evil.

"Don't say that. You'll bring unhappiness to pass."

"It's painful losing you."

"My mother taught me that worldly things are transient.

Love dies from lack of nourishment."

Geoff perked up on the mention of love. Matilda leapt to quash any budding hope.

"A figure of speech." She grinned. "You're incorrigible."

She lounged against a mossy tree trunk and asked, "Why come into the forest to play music? You have a luxurious manor."

"But no peace," he replied in disgust. "My sister is making my home miserable."

"Still suspicious?"

"She can't get it through her head that I'm respecting your choice of William. She accuses me—as if she reads my heart instead of hearing my words."

He put the recorder to his lips, but stopped before playing.

"Rosamund doesn't understand that I don't want to drive you from Caelfield. While you live here with William I can see you—speak with you."

Matilda looked more comfortable as if a burden had been lifted from her shoulders.

"We should talk of other things," she said. "Play a happy tune."

"If playing happy tunes will keep you near, I will."

As if forgetting her earlier resolve, she crossed the clearing and sat on the boulder. Soon her foot was tapping and she was singing. Sometimes he stopped playing and added his baritone to her alto. They joked about lyrics—they laughed when notes went sour. Time passed. A bond budded, drawing them closer together.

"It's fun being with someone my own age," he heard her say. He wanted desperately to stroke the nape of her neck, but resisted. Even in old, dirty clothes, she drew him to her.

She gasped when she glanced at the angle of the sun.

"Oh, no! Look how low the sun is. I'm late."

She jumped up, grabbing her basket in a rush to leave.

"If I run, I can get home to set out William's meal."

Geoff felt stunned—as if rudely awakened from a deep and highly pleasurable dream.

"Come back tomorrow," he pleaded as she pushed her way out of the clearing.

"I'll try." She flung the words over her shoulder as she fled.

Matilda chided herself as she stumbled along.

"I should've kept watch on the hour."

Just when she needed to be her most sure footed, her feet seemed to be their most uncertain. The undergrowth—that seemed minimal on her trip into the forest—now seemed to have found a way to position itself into her path. She became frustrated by her slow progress.

"Nature conspires against me."

She pushed ruthlessly through the restraining vegetation. She needed to pick up the duties of everyday life—to push this brief interlude from her mind. She arrived at the cottage out of breath. William was already there, seated, his meal on the table.

"Where have you been?"

Matilda heard the worry behind his words and felt terrible to be the cause of it. She sagged against the back of a chair and gulped in lungsful of air until she could reply.

"I went mushrooming. The baron was in the woods, playing a recorder. I stopped to thank him for saving us from Sir Loric and to ask about his wounds. I listened to his tunes for awhile and lost track of time."

"Why did you stay to listen?"

His voice had an edge to it.

Matilda couldn't answer, because she didn't know herself why she had lingered.

Chapter Twenty-One

Matilda heard the music while still far away.

She'd brought a basket for mushrooms, but didn't pause to gather any. If she'd asked herself why, she would've answered that Geoff must know without delay about William's anger at their chance meeting yesterday. It was the excuse she gave herself when she hurried from the cottage that morning. Now, hearing the sound of the recorder, she felt drawn to the clearing for a different reason.

As she stepped through the overlapping branches, the delicate aroma of dogwood seemed more compelling today—the patch of grass extra green. Nearby, song birds chirped.

Matilda noticed how Geoff's finely woven tunic fit his muscled body, how his golden pendant sparkled as it lay exposed to the sun. He'd dressed more carefully today. His feet—encased in calf-clinging boots—were firmly planted on the ground, presenting a confidence he didn't possess yesterday.

She, on the other hand, wore the same dull garment as the day before—not her first choice, but the logical choice when collecting mushrooms. She could little afford to ruin her better clothing. Besides, if seen, she didn't want gossip to start because she was clothed inappropriately.

While dressing that morning, Matilda realized her attitude had done a turnabout. For her first trip to the manor, she'd deliberately chosen her ugliest clothing. Today, she wished it could be the opposite.

As she placed her mushrooming basket on the grass, Geoff set his recorder on the boulder and crossed the clearing. He clasped her hands and Matilda wondered if he noticed the calluses.

"I'm glad you came. I feared you wouldn't."

"William doesn't want me near you."

Geoff grinned boyishly.

"I don't blame him. If I were William, I'd keep you far away from me."

He released her hands, breaking the bond she'd felt.

"How long can you stay?"

She'd intended to say she couldn't stay. Even as she answered, she knew she was taking a step into danger.

"For two songs."

"I'll make them the longest songs I know."

Geoff returned to the boulder and took up his recorder. As if following a preordained script, she sat herself beside him. She let the music wrap around her. It danced along her skin and brought joy. When the two songs ended, she sighed before sliding off the boulder and picking up her basket. She had responsibilities.

"I need to get mushrooms and get home. I neglected my work yesterday and it's piled up."

Geoff rose, tucking the recorder into his embroidered tunic.

"Let me help you dig mushrooms."

She couldn't imagine dragging those embroidered sleeves in the dirt.

"You'll get dirty."

"I can bathe. My clothes will be washed for me."

"What if someone sees us?"

"We'll hear them coming. I'm not engrossed in misery like yesterday when you sneaked up on me. Besides, I'm a lord. I can do what I want."

"True. I'll be the one condemned."

Geoff appeared to sober at her remark, but he didn't let up on the pressure. She resisted half-heartedly. After agreeing, she puzzled at the change in herself from just a few weeks ago.

Upon arrival at a nearby patch, she taught him to identify the mushrooms, handle and pack them. Some she would dry for herbal remedies and soup stock. Others she would use for meals. As they knelt side by side in the moist soil, the pendant around Geoff's neck slipped out from under his shirt and caught the rays of the small amount of sun invading the dense forest. Matilda imagined tucking it back inside.

"You're the first person since childhood to have me grubbing in the dirt."

"A little dirt is good for you," she said with a grin. "It'll bring you off of your high horse."

He grinned back.

"You and my sister are the only two women to talk back to me. The rest have no backbone."

After working a second patch, Geoff said. "I believe this year I'll join in the harvest. Digging in dirt is fun."

"You'll soon change your mind," she told him. "After a few hours bent over, your calves will cramp and your back will seem to have grown a hump."

Geoff laughed, throwing his arms wide.

"I'll think twice before becoming a farmer."

His recorder slipped from his tunic. He and Matilda

grabbed for it and bumped heads—hard. Geoff deliberately staggered around—hands clamped to his head, pretending to be knocked into silliness. Matilda—seeing stars herself—laughed and joined in. It felt good to shed responsibilities—to act like a child. Her heart beat faster as he walked toward her.

"Here, let me massage that bump I gave you. No need to get a headache."

Matilda's breath caught as his fingers found their way through the tight curls to her scalp. She knew she should pull away. Instead, she positioned his fingers on the painful spot and closed her eyes to the massage transmitting a sensual message onto her skin. She stood, relishing the sensations spreading toward her loins. When he abruptly pulled away, she felt abandoned.

"I'd better stop now or I'll not be able to stop."

Geoff spoke jokingly, but she heard the seriousness beneath.

Matilda pretended to be unaffected, hoping that the weakness in her knees wouldn't give her away.

"Quite right. We'd better finish up. I have other chores to do before my husband gets home."

She needed to remind them both of William. She had yet to speak the words to release her cousin from his family obligation and send herself home to Wroxton.

With Geoff working at her side, Matilda quickly had enough mushrooms to use for upcoming meals and to dry for balm. She gathered up her basket to return to the cottage.

"May I walk with you?"

She nodded, incapable of denying him.

Geoff relieved her of her basket as she started homeward through a forest not yet fully penetrated by the heat of the day.

While keeping a distance between themselves in case they were observed, they discussed favorite fabrics, colors, music, the fair, birds, gardening and people as they walked. Geoff asked for the reasons behind her choices. She warmed to the realization that he was interested enough to ask her.

"I'm thinking of visiting Dunavik next week," she blurted out.

"I'll show you some of my mother's favorite gowns while you're there. Her tastes matched yours."

"I'd like that."

"What day will you visit?"

"Monday morning after William leaves for work."

"Good."

Matilda realized she'd committed herself to a dangerous scheme. She started to protest that it was Dunavik she intended to visit, but they had arrived at the path to the manor where Geoff would leave her. As he returned her basket, he bent quickly and kissed her. Before she knew it, he was gone, humming as he walked while her ears buzzed and her face burned.

She glanced around, worried, but no one had seen that kiss.

Chapter Twenty-Two

By the time of her cousin's early return from the forest that evening, Matilda had her heavy work done and was embroidering in a chair she'd placed outside the open cottage door. As she greeted him, she noticed his distress.

"What's the matter, William?"

"Flcher got injured today. His axe slipped. We stopped the bleeding, but I worry the wound will open up again when we move him. Will you come with me to sew it?"

"Of course. Where is he?"

"About twenty minutes down the path."

"Was he wearing an amulet to protect against evil?"

William shook his head.

"Flcher is moving away from the Saxon beliefs of healing the spirit along with the body."

"Unfortunate," Matilda replied over her shoulder as she went to the shelf where she stored her Simple Chest containing the herbs. "He'll heal faster if he has his wound sung to while the poultice is applied. Luckily, tonight's a full moon. It adds extra healing force to the charm poems."

Matilda checked the level of the nine-herbs powder made from mugwort, plantain, lamb's cress, cock's-spur grass, chamomile, nettle, crab-apple, chervil and fennel. She checked the powders to aid healing and the one to reduce pain. "I'll need the juice of two apples, William."

While he was gone to the root cellar, Matilda checked the rest of her supplies. Her containers were clean and she had enough bindings and ties. After William returned with the apples, she cut them into small sections and dropped the pieces into the center of her metal funnel sieve around which she had tied a piece of cheesecloth. She used her wooden pestle to grind. The juice seeped through the small holes into the bowl underneath, straining through the cheesecloth.

Matilda put the dirty sieve and cloth to the side while she mixed some powders into a measured amount of juice. Then she grated soap into the bowl and stirred this mixture until it all became a paste. Once the salve was ready, she put it into a small wooden bowl, put on its wooden top and tied it all securely with a string. She placed it carefully into the Simple Chest.

"William, is there water out by Flcher?"

"Yes, my pig's bladder is still there."

"What about ale?"

"We have lots of that as well. Are you ready?"

"Yes."

William picked up the chest and carried it out the door toward the forest path. Matilda grabbed her cloak from the peg by the door and the two blankets she had set out. She wrapped the drawstring of the cloth bag containing the bandages and ties around her wrist and hurried after William, carefully closing the cottage door behind her.

Soon Matilda knelt at Flcher's side. William set her chest nearby while she untied the strip of cloth that bound a larger cloth to the wound. Dried blood was making sections of it stick.

"How are you, Flcher?"

"I'll make it," he reassured Matilda through clenched teeth.

"Give me that water, William. And give Flcher all the ale you have," she ordered as she tied a tourniquet to the upper leg to make sure the blood wouldn't start flowing when she removed the bandaging.

A younger worker brought out his pouch of ale to add to William's supply and Flcher took huge swallows.

"Someone wrap one of these blankets around him to keep him warm. We don't want you to catch a chill, Flcher," she joked, "not when I'm going to all this trouble to patch you up."

Matilda trickled water along the edges until she could gently lift off the cloth where it had stuck to the wound. The men had used a patch torn from Flcher's pants after they removed them, where the material had already been damaged by the axe. This cloth was coarser and less clean than that of his shirt, but Matilda could understand not wanting to cut up a perfectly good shirt if something else would suffice.

"Start making a stretcher out of this second blanket while I work on this wound," she directed the men.

She poured water into a small pitcher she took out of the chest. To this she added some ginger and turmeric herbs and poured the herbal mixture over the wound to cleanse it. She then dipped white gauze into the solution and cleaned the surrounding skin. The turmeric would stain, but staining was preferable to allowing pus to form.

"You're lucky. The axe cut only the skin, not the deep layers to the bone. But I need to sew this together."

Matilda found her needle and catgut thread. All her skill in delicate sewing would be needed to close this wound so that it would leave no ugly scar.

"Stay close, William. I'll need you to hold his leg steady while I stitch. Someone light a torch and hold it close, please. These trees make it too dark for fine work." She looked at her patient. "Are you ready?"

He nodded sloppily, showing his inebriation.

Matilda gathered the flesh together and worked with steady concentration.

"I'm finished. Now, more salve to keep pus from forming."

As she applied the salve, Matilda sang a refrain from nine-herbs charm song. "The snake came crawling and struck at none. But Woden took nine glory twigs and struck the adder so that it flew into nine parts." When she finished, she noticed Flcher was more relaxed, even if he professed to no longer believe in the old ways.

Matilda released the tourniquet, pleased no blood leaked through her stitching onto the white pad and salve she'd placed against the wound. She wrapped bandages around Flcher's calf and secured them in place.

"Be sure to eat plenty of green vegetables, carrots and pumpkin seeds to help with the healing. And stay off that leg for a while. Give yourself a chance to heal."

"We'll get you home," William said. He turned to the others. "We can trade off carrying the stretcher. Are you ready?"

They lifted Flcher onto the make-shift stretcher. As they neared the cutoff to the cottage, Matilda said, "I'll go straight home, William. I know my way."

"I'll stay with Flcher to see him settled in."

Back at the cottage, as she put her Simple Chest away, Matilda reviewed in her head the actions she took for the injured man and felt content she'd done the right things.

She walked to the cooking shed, added wood to the fire and put the soup on to heat. The coolness of early evening settled on her, but it wasn't chilly enough to get out a shawl for warmth. Still, one thing chilled her. In the excitement of Flcher's injury, she never told William about today's mushrooming and Monday's trip to the manor house.

When William returned, she was sitting outside the cottage door using the last light of the day to do her embroidering. "Your meal is ready. Do you want to eat?"

"I will."

"Do you mind if I finish this section of embroidery while I have some daylight? I'll get your soup now, but eat later."

"Fine," William said as he slumped tiredly in the other chair.

She headed to the cooking shed to ladle out the soup and get some bread and ale. As she brought them to the table, William washed his hands and forearms in the basin by the door and dried them on the piece of cloth hanging from a peg.

"How is Flcher?"

"He has pain, but no fever. His neighbor is keeping an eye on him."

He settled in to eat. He ate in silence and Matilda did nothing to disturb that silence. While he was tending to his friend, she'd decided not talk about her promise to go to the manor.

She worked her needle until it was too dark to see the pattern and then brought her embroidery into the cottage to store in a chest. She sat down across at the table from William with a bowl of soup.

"You're quiet tonight, Matilda. Did working on Flcher tire

143

you?"

"Yes," she lied.

Anxiety about her trip to the manor Monday morning was eating at her.

"I think I'll go to bed early."

"I'll go back to Flcher to make sure he has everything he needs for the night. You get your rest."

Matilda washed the dishes and brought the chair back inside. She checked one last time on the cow and pigs and made sure the kitten was securely locked in for the night. She closed the chicken coop door against predators.

As she climbed under the bed covers, her mind was uneasy about not telling William about her visit to the manor three days hence. When he returned much later, she pretended to be asleep.

Chapter Twenty-Three

Monday morning, Dunavik was waiting outside, eliminating the chance that someone else would answer her knock. The chatelaine leaned against the manor wall, her arms tightly folded across her broad bosom. Those folded arms spoke to Matilda.

"You're making a bad mistake."

A lump of unease formed in Matilda's throat. She loosened the collar of her cloak.

"This is nothing more than a visit. I've come to see you— and some of his mother's clothing."

Dunavik wagged her finger.

"There's no use pretending you came to see me."

"But…"

"If anyone asks, I'll lie through my teeth and say you did, but why cause trouble for that dear husband of yours?"

Guilt thoroughly dissolved Matilda's resolve.

"You're right. I should return home."

When she started to retreat, Dunavik caught her arm.

"Wait. If the baron learns you got all the way to this door and I sent you back home, there'll be hell to pay. You'd better explain things to him."

Matilda nodded. She hoped she'd have the willpower to go home once she laid eyes on Geoff.

The chatelaine released her arm, but cautioned her, "Once inside, don't speak. Keep your face averted from doorways. Lady Rosamund is still in her chambers and I gave the upstairs servants chores in other parts of the manor, but you never know."

Dunavik opened the rear door, looked about and beckoned to her.

Matilda, her head down, followed the serviceable, grey kirtle skirt along the familiar corridor toward the back stairs. Smells of food and laundry wafted into the hallway. The clatter of pots and the voices of kitchen staff drifted along the passageway.

They climbed the stairs and walked the paneled corridor toward the mother's bedchamber. Neither noticed Keridwen, whose eyes watched them with malice.

Matilda stood just inside the door Dunavik had firmly shut behind her. Geoff crossed the wood planked floor, a broad smile on his face. Indeed, if he were a puppy's tail, he'd be wagging at full speed. It made it harder to get out what she needed to say.

"I shouldn't have come," she began hesitantly, wringing her hands. "Something got in the way of my good sense. I must go home."

"Never say that."

Despite his reply, Geoff didn't look surprised. He rested his hands lightly on her shoulders.

"You're a guest in my home."

"But I had to skulk up the back steps."

"For your protection."

She felt drawn into a spider's web toward which she had

willingly traveled. She removed his hands and stepped back.

"All this hiding tells me this is wrong."

He grasped her hands.

"Stay. At least for an hour."

Her head shook in the negative, but she said, "All right."

A grin of pure joy highlighted the boy in him and downplayed the dangerous man she knew could rise to the surface in a flash.

Now that the die was cast, Matilda looked hesitantly around. Shutters opened to the sunshine's warmth and the freshness of the meadow, giving the room a welcoming aura. Richly appointed, the chamber held an armoire, a bed of dark oak and several wooden chests with deep carvings. Tapestries of burnt orange, gold and rich red-browns decorated its walls. She delighted in the quality of the hand work.

Splits of wood and dried tinder lay in the hearth. Since no one lived in these rooms, she assumed a fire was lit periodically to keep the damp from damaging the furnishings. On a table sat a vase of meadow flowers, adding color and fragrance. A repast of sweetmeats and wine was set out on an inlaid table in front of the hearth. Geoff gestured toward it.

"Are you hungry?"

She shook her head.

The back of his hand brushed her cheek and seemed to brand her.

"Your cheeks are rosy."

"From the fresh air," she lied. They were flushed because of his nearness.

"I'm happy you're here."

As he talked, he unfastened her blue coif. Although she'd pushed his hands away, he'd already succeeded in freeing her turbulent curls.

Without warning, he lifted her high and swung her in an exuberant circle. When he set her down, she resolutely removed his hands from her waist.

"If you take liberties again, I'm going home."

His eyes sparkled and he had a lopsided grin.

"You have my promise."

He looked unrepentant.

"Let me show you around. My mother loved this chamber."

He pointed to a wall hanging of three stunning tapestries by the weavers of Flanders. The artist in Matilda rose to the surface as she studied them. One showed a scene from court, one a family in a garden setting hosting their tenants at a festival supper and the last was a coat of arms.

"An artisan brought sketches to the manor. My mother chose these two designs representing our dual responsibility to king and tenants. The coat of arms is ours."

He urged her to feel the depth of the carving to the chests.

"My mother bought these in London. They were carved by Italian craftsmen."

He pointed out the skill needed to align the lid with the box and its hinges.

She ran her hand along the seam.

"Skillful like William."

Geoff seemed to flinch, then shrug it off.

She was feeling overwhelmed as he guided her to windows opening onto lush lawns flowing down the hill to the edge of the forest and kept low by tethered goats. There was such a monetary divide between her and Geoff.

Cattle and sheep grazed in distance pastures. Farmlands of

plowed, black earth dotted the landscape. Sounds drifted through the window as villagers went about the work of caring for the soil. She could see William's cottage peeping through the trees—the front door fully visible—and wondered if Geoff ever spied on her from here.

Her cousin was such a large part of her life that, even here, he occupied her thoughts.

"Look there." Geoff leaned out of the window.

Matilda positioned herself at his side even though his nearness was disturbing. Her eyes followed the line of his outstretched finger to a mill paddlewheel slowly turning from the pressure of creek water made stronger by a small dam.

"I had that waterwheel put in shortly after I took over the estate. The water does the work oxen used to do. And if we have a low rainfall, we still have the oxen to fall back on.

"And there."

He pointed to pastureland just before the horizon.

"Most of our calves and lambs survive birth. Our herds have increased threefold these past years and our wool is superior. We sell a sheep for five pennies when the average price is three."

The immense size of the tithe barn was evidence of the fertility of this land.

"You have much to be proud of. William speaks well of you."

A shadow crossed Geoff's face for a second time on hearing her cousin's name.

He drew her across the room and flung open the armoire's doors to reveal gowns of cottons, linens and velvets in beautiful colors with silver and gold thread and fur trim.

"They were my mother's, as was the one you wore the first

night you were here."

This time it was Matilda's turn to flinch.

"What do you think?"

She reached in to caress the lush folds of velvet and the crisp linen. If she became Geoff's mistress, she would wear these.

"They're beautiful."

He pulled a velvet gown from the armoire and pressed it against her.

"Hold this up."

She couldn't resist the lure of that lush softness of emerald green with its red-brown fox trim. She buried her hands in the fur and held it to her face.

"Stunning," he whispered, not clarifying if he meant the gown or her. "Are you certain I can't entice you to live with me?"

She handed the garment to him.

"I'm certain."

But not certain in her heart.

He threw it onto the bed. One after the other the garments were pulled out of the armoire, held up to Matilda and thrown onto the bed.

"All these lovely garments are in a heap."

"The servants will take care of them."

Geoff opened a chest to reveal a treasure trove of colorful cloaks, headgear, buckles, pins, ribbons and scarves. He removed a gold jewelry casket from a locked metal chest and held it out to her.

"I can't touch that. What if something turns up missing? I'd be labeled a thief." She thrust his hands away. "Put it back."

He started to open the casket lid.

"Don't even show them to me. I don't want to know what's in there."

Looking crestfallen, he replaced the unopened casket in its heavy metal chest. He dropped the key back into the pouch that hung from his belt and sat on a leather chair nearby.

"Try on anything you want."

"You just want to catch me half-dressed," she said jokingly as she carefully returned each gown to a peg in the armoire.

Geoff pushed himself up. He gestured toward the food laid out.

"Leave those. Eat something with me."

Matilda shook her head.

"I must leave. I've neglected my chores long enough."

"When will I see you again?" he asked.

The chamber door burst open, startling Geoff. His sister, still dressed in bedclothes, rushed in—face red—breath coming in short bursts. She slammed the door shut and screeched, "Why is this woman in our mother's chambers?"

Rosamund reached out to attack Matilda with hands like claws, but he stepped in between and blocked her with his body. He grabbed the outstretched hands, twisting them away from his face.

"You're the intruder. Get out!"

Rosamund tore away and—flailing her arms—stomped around the chamber.

"What can you be thinking of to bring this low-born into our mother's chambers?"

Anger pulsed through him.

"Hold your tongue."

"When will you learn the dignity of your **position?**" his sister screeched. "My Maximilian could teach you a few things."

"It may be time for you to return to your husband. You're certainly doing no good for my household."

His sister faced him, hands on her hips, fury on her face.

"I can't understand you. There are women enough of your own social standing who would love to be invited to see these chambers."

Geoff's patience was losing the battle with reining in his temper.

"How did you know Matilda was here?"

"Keridwen told me that female sneaked in here."

"This woman has a name. She also has a reputation. You and Keridwen will not besmirch it."

"She's Anglo-Saxon."

"As is most everyone else on my estates. These were their lands."

"She's a commoner."

"Related to the wife of an earl."

"She's dung and I'll prove it."

"If you try, I'll lock you away until I can send you home to your Maximilian. And Keridwen will be flogged and exiled. Make sure she knows that."

His sister paled.

"You defend that low-born over your own sister!"

"I do," Geoff replied. "I'll send you back to your husband."

Rosamund looked into his eyes and must have seen nothing there to benefit her. She fell silent. For all the touted good qualities of her husband, Geoff knew it was Maximilian's bad qualities that his wife sought to escape during these lengthy visits to her ancestral home. Marriage had turned his intelligent and beautiful sister into a spiteful shrew. He no longer could find the sweet girl of his youth under that hard shell of arrogance.

Geoff waited while his sister visibly regained control. She lifted her chin.

"I'll not say a word about her being here," she eventually replied, no longer shouting, "neither will Keridwen." She shook a finger at Matilda. "But you keep that low-born out of my mother's chambers!"

Rosamund sailed out the door, slamming it behind her.

Humiliated and drained, Matilda's happy mood was utterly shattered. A dark, heavy sadness for things-not-to-be weighed on her.

"I shouldn't have come. I set myself up for this."

"Rosamund is the one who wronged you," Geoff countered as he crossed the floor toward her. "As my guest, you shouldn't be subjected to her tirades."

"I want to go home."

Matilda could think of no other place she'd rather be than in her cottage surrounded by the familiar, placid atmosphere William had created there.

"That seems best."

Geoff took her gently into his arms and held her close for a few minutes. His breath caressed her cheek. An aroma of soap and leather so distinctive of him encircled her until he set her away.

"Stay here. I'll send for Dunavik."

He left through a side door that she saw opened directly into his bedchamber.

A sharp pain squeezed her heart. This chamber would belong to Geoff's future wife. To these rooms he would freely come and go. Her only offer was as mistress—a woman set aside from the eyes of society.

She tried to put the day into perspective, but the scales wouldn't balance—tipping to the negative. She'd learned a powerful lesson—put yourself in compromising circumstances and you get pummeled!

She must stay away from Geoff while she resolved her situation with her cousin and she could return to Wroxton.

Dunavik bustled in, her grey skirts sweeping the floor. She cut right to the heart of the matter.

"Lord Geoff told me of Lady Rosamund's tantrum. I wish, now, I had let you go home when you wanted to leave."

Matilda shrugged her shoulders.

"Wisdom comes with experience—usually bad experiences like this one."

"You can't fault yourself for being young and inexperienced."

Dunavik sounded like the mother Matilda sorely missed, whose practical wisdom meant so much.

She waited while Dunavik checked the corridor and then followed her down the back stairs and out the tradesmen's door. As far as she could tell, she escaped unseen.

Chapter Twenty-Four

The baron was speaking with his overseer as they rode toward a distant field.

"She's the first woman whose eyes don't glaze over when I talk about the estate and its people. She's intelligent and grasps what I'm trying to accomplish."

"I'll give her that much," Voernulf said.

"Then Lady Rosamund burst in and ruined it all."

"You flirt with danger. I advise you against more trysts."

Geoff's heart was heavy. There seemed no resolution to its ache.

"Matilda struck me like a flash of lightning. I'm still blinded."

"When you attend court this winter, you can find a good Norman woman to take as wife."

Geoff grimaced. His future looked bitter.

Although the cottage air was warmer than when she left this morning, Matilda found herself shivering. The chill planted by Lady Rosamund couldn't be warmed in the sun.

She got out the ale and bread, went to the root cellar for some cheese, then to the cookhouse for a plate. A woodpecker beat out a rhythm that followed her in and out of doorways. She wondered if Geoff watched her from his mother's chamber window.

On one of her trips, the kitten followed her through the open doorway and into the cottage.

"My Fate, I enjoyed being with Geoff today. I was fascinated when he talked about his estate. It raised hopes we could be friends."

The kitten made a sound that seemed like denial.

"I know. I know. I'm being naive."

The kitten brushed against her, its soft black and white fur rubbing against her skirts in apparent agreement.

"And then his sister ruined things."

Still, she couldn't stop herself from hoping.

"Is it impossible to just be friends with him?"

The kitten turned its back, tail held high, and strolled out the door.

"A lot of help you are," Matilda called after it, seeing the unsettled future predicted by the fortuneteller looming before her.

Five days later Matilda and William rose early to tend to the animals so they could take their extra eggs to market. She also planned to sell several embroidered handkerchiefs, two tablecloths and a blouse with colorful stitching.

The eggs were carefully packed and the embroidery was in its own basket to keep it from getting soiled. She packed a large cloth for them to sit on. She tied some bread for mid-day meal into another cloth and filled a bladder with spring water. A hint of a breeze wafted through the open door. While she waited for William to finish feeding the animals, she shelled some peas to add to the soup stock and snapped the ends off string beans. If she had time, she'd get a knife from the cooking shed to peel potatoes.

She was humming one of the tunes Geoff had played on his recorder when William walked in. She hadn't told him about her trip to the manor on Monday. She still hadn't made plans to return to Wroxton. Everywhere she looked she found reasons to stay.

"Are you ready?"

"I am. Would you like a mug of ale before we leave?"

"Yes. You spoil me."

"It's my pleasure."

As Matilda passed his chair, she briefly put her hand on his back, admiring the strength in his shoulders as she did so. Although there were many good qualities about her cousin, she now knew her fleeting thought that she could settle for companionship was utterly foolish.

When William was ready, they gathered up the baskets and walked toward the village for the market.

"What was that song you were humming?"

"It's a song about a wandering minstrel who falls in love with a woman from the south country. He's destined to be apart from his love because her family won't let her wander with him."

"It's a sad song."

She felt a kinship with the lovers.

"They have accepted the circumstances and only meet a few times a year."

At the market, Matilda spread the cloth under a shady elm and laid out the eggs. She paid particular attention to the placement of her embroidery with its bright thread and intricate patterns. Embroidery of Anglo-Saxon design was becoming so popular it was being exported to Normandy.

She and William had been sitting only a few minutes when a male acquaintance approached. Always disheveled, today his beard needed trimming and his clothes smelled of his occupation as a herder.

"I saw you at the manor on Monday taking leave of Dunavik—about mid-day."

Matilda's throat constricted. Her stomach flip-flopped while she tried to appear unflustered.

"Oh? I didn't see you. Where were you?"

"I was crossing the grounds. I was staking the goats to a new patch of grass."

He grinned and Matilda could see a gap where he'd lost two teeth. The grin was natural, uncalculating. She relaxed.

"Give a shout next time."

"You looked in a hurry, but next time I will. I wanted to tell you I'm impressed with your healing skills. We're hoping you'll take over when Mother Nellis gives up the practice."

They leisurely discussed Flcher's recovery and then he moved on to talk with others. When he left, William looked askance at her, but didn't confront her about the trip to the manor.

She heard a horse stop a short time later, while she was resting her eyes. She looked up, her heart sinking. Lady Rosamund. The woman held Matilda's spirit in bondage.

A stable lad rode with her, but none of her ladies-in-waiting. Impressively, her scarlet riding gown had a stitched bodice of silver thread. Her horse's bridle and saddle shone with inlaid silver.

Lady Rosamund drew herself up in the saddle, took a deep breath and demanded in a haughty tone, "Give me one of those handkerchiefs."

The stable boy dismounted and picked one.

"No, the one with green edging."

Never satisfied until she set the terms, Geoff's sister was playing her usual games. Matilda remained mute. Rosamund flipped a coin in her direction. It landed in the dirt.

"I assume that will pay for it."

"It does," William responded without even looking at the coin. He stepped in front of Matilda and glared at the baron's sister.

Lady Rosamund took the exquisitely stitched handkerchief from the stable lad. With calm deliberation, she dropped it onto the ground. A white cloth fluttering so close to its head was not to her horse's liking. It shied, stamping the handkerchief deeply into the dirt. Matilda felt as if this woman was grinding her into the mud as well.

The stable boy reached for it, but Lady Rosamund stopped him. "Don't bother. It's too crude to be worth anything."

She turned the horse and slowly rode off—head held high, eyes gleaming—without revealing the secret visit, although hinting of her power over Matilda because of it. The boy hurried after her.

William shrugged, then picked up the handkerchief and folded it.

"We'll get it washed. It's not torn."

"I don't want to see it again. Not after that woman touched it."

"Don't waste a thing of beauty because of spitefulness. People saw what happened. Show them Lady Rosamund's cruelty doesn't bother us."

"But it does. Now that Sir Loric is dead, I should return to

Wroxton."

"Perhaps it would be best."

Chapter Twenty-Five

In the still of the early hours, the morning after Lady Rosamund's outrageous behavior at the market, Matilda went to the spring for water. As she started down the path, swinging her bucket, she heard the lilting tones of a recorder. Briefly, she thought of returning to the cottage and barring the door. Yet, the sound drew her to him today as easily as those other days in the forest.

As she stepped from the path onto the grass by the spring, Geoff slipped the recorder into his tunic. "I hoped you'd come."

"I almost turned back."

"I had no way to prevent my sister from hurting you yesterday."

"I've learned that you wouldn't harm me in that spiteful way."

"Will you stay with me a while?"

"For a little."

Matilda rinsed the bucket and then tipped it into the spring's pool. When it was full, she placed it on a rock at the edge of the stream's bed.

"Leave your bucket and come with me," Geoff said. "There's a glade a short way from here. This spring is too close to the path for privacy."

Matilda abandoned her bucket and followed him. He pushed through the brush until they came to a patch of meadow grass obscured from prying eyes. He turned and took her into his arms, kissing the nape of her neck.

"We shouldn't," she quietly protested, although she didn't push him away.

"I've been so worried about you. I can't sleep."

"I'm learning to cope." Her heart wrenched as she said, "I'm returning to my family in Wroxton."

"No! When?"

"When William can find the time from his obligations to take me. Our life in Caelfield has been a mistake. I'll go home."

His face registered such dismay that she reached out to soothe the furrows of pain from his forehead. He captured her hand, kissed it and held it against his cheek.

"I'll never see you again."

The pain in his voice brought tears to her eyes.

"It must be so."

He enfolded her in his arms and she clung to him as to a lifeline. His fingers tangled in her hair as he clasped her head to his shoulder. Matilda could feel his heart beating. Their love reached out to one another.

"Come. Let me love you," Geoff whispered into her hair. "One last time."

"I vowed to stay away from you."

"I can't deny myself."

She didn't object.

He spread his finely woven tunic on the spring growth and untied her shawl of rough cloth—which dropped obligingly to the grass. Heat surged through her as his hands found the ties and belts securing her outer garments. Releasing them, he exposed her white linen shift to his view. This, too, he opened to reveal her body to his touch.

She moaned as Geoff ran his fingers along her breast. He stroked the taut flesh, evoking fierce stirrings in her loins, even as his mouth found hers. Clinging to her lips desperately, he struggled to remove his clothing. When these interfering garments fell away to the accommodating grass, he lifted her and placed her tenderly on his tunic, then slipped easily to the earth beside her.

"You draw me to you like a moth to a flame."

"You're the melody that runs through my life," she murmured. "My body sings whenever you are near."

He pressed his nakedness to hers. She became exquisitely aware of the fullness of her breasts against his hard, muscled chest, the brute strength in his thighs.

She wrapped her legs tightly around him, opening herself to him, absorbing him into her depths and engulfing him in the eternal rhythm of love, until he cried out. They climaxed as one and slid easily into a languid exhaustion.

Holding each other, they waited while their breathing quieted. The sounds of nearby insects and birds penetrated their glade and brought encroaching reality.

"My sweet. We've been foolish. And yet, I cannot regret it."

"Nor I."

She lightly slid her fingers along his chest, disturbing the tiny hairs and re-evoking strong urgings inside her.

"Come stay with me."

"Not as your mistress."

She couldn't endure the ostracism it would bring.

He ran a finger off the edge of her nose and let it linger on

163

her upper lip. She captured and suckled it.

Geoff rose to one elbow, watching her.

"I've never felt this way before. I love you desperately."

"If I were released from my vows, would you marry me?"

His face twisted into a grimace.

"You know I can't. I must marry to protect the estates."

"Being a mistress bars me from decent society. Is that the life you want for me?"

He hung his head, unhappiness awash on his face.

"Of course not."

"Nor do I."

"I'm being pushed to secure the inheritance. If I bring a wife home from winter court, you'd be exiled. No new bride would tolerate a mistress close at hand."

She started gathering up her clothing, shaking off bits of debris that clung.

"William and I aren't announcing the end to our marriage until he returns from Wroxton."

She still held on to the pretend marriage as a barrier between them.

"He'll pack my things and send them later."

"I'll pay to have them transported to Wroxton."

"That relieves me of a burden. I've cost William so much."

"It's a small thing I can easily do."

"We'll stay at least through the annual masquerade. To leave before then would stir up too many questions."

"Perhaps in costume under cover of darkness I can dance with you."

She stood to leave, wrapping her cloak around her.

"I'll go now."

He flopped back onto the grass and pressed his hands against his forehead as if trying to relieve a splitting headache.

"If letting you go means your happiness, then I release you."

Immense sadness washed over her.

"Not happiness, Geoff, but wellbeing and purpose. That must be enough."

Before pushing through the brush at the edge of the glade, she turned for one last look at the love she must leave behind. Matilda felt a momentary chill, as if someone were walking on her grave.

Chapter Twenty-Six

Matilda was walking into Caelfield a few days later when she heard a shout. She turned and saw Carnulf running toward her wearing his usual mischievous grin. She slowed her pace so he could catch up. The day was cooling and the crickets had started their nighttime chorus.

"You look nice."

She had freshened up after clearing the evening meal—dressing in a blue kirtle of finer weave than her everyday garment.

"Thank you."

Carnulf was still in work clothes and grubby with sweat from the heat of the forge.

"Where are you going?"

"To Berwyn's."

He circled Matilda, hopping from foot to foot.

"May I tag along?"

She nodded and he fell into step beside her. Every so often he did a skip or a hop, as if a normal stroll was beyond him. Although they were almost the same age, she felt much more mature. These past months had forced her to grow up quickly.

Carnulf began kicking pebbles back and forth between his boots as he walked. Despite his physically hard job, he seemed to make play time out of every opportunity.

"I made my costume for the masquerade next weekend," he said. "What are you wearing?"

"I haven't decided yet. Probably a monk's cloak."

"It's the best festival of the year. There's lots of food. And at dark, there are bonfires and dancing—like at the fair, except everyone is costumed and masked." He grinned. "We're a lot freer when we don't know who's on the other side of the mask."

Matilda took a swipe at the stone, risking a scuff mark on her soft boots.

"You'll never guess my costume," he said.

"You're right. I can't guess."

"A satyr."

Matilda laughed.

"A lecherous wood deity is just the costume for you. I'll be certain to save a dance for the satyr."

When they arrived at Berwyn's, he turned away toward the smithy and the finish of his day's work. He walked off, whistling.

Matilda was soon seated at the table with ale and sweetmeats. Berwyn wore drab work clothes, but her cheerful personality put life and color into whatever clothing she hung on her body.

"You outshine me today. What's the occasion?"

"No occasion. I felt the need to dress up."

Feeling good about herself filled the hole where Geoff was cut out.

"I hear Lady Rosamund made a scene at the market the other day."

"She's a thorn in my side. She singles me out for her

spitefulness."

"I wonder what started it."

Matilda would not go so far as revealing the original source—her night with Geoff.

"She made a snide remark about Saxons at the fair. I made one just as loudly about her lack of manners. Ever since then, she's had it in for me."

Berwyn threw her head back and laughed.

"You didn't!"

Matilda hung her head sheepishly.

"I did. Sometimes my tongue speaks before my mind thinks."

Berwyn shook her head, looking disgusted.

"That woman has gotten worse since her marriage. My advice is to stay out of her way."

"I will. And you must help me."

Berwyn nodded vigorously. "What can I do?"

Heads together, they made plans for ways to avoid the baron's sister at the masquerade.

When Matilda rose to go home, Berwyn said, "Stowig and I will be your second pair of eyes. You can count on us."

As she walked to William's cottage, sadness overwhelmed her. She'd made good friends in Caelfield. She'd soon leave them—with no opportunity for final goodbyes.

Chapter Twenty-Seven

Early evening of the masquerade, William's ox cart was filled with elders and friends—just like on the night of the banquet.

The cart's rocking movement soothed Matilda. This motion that rocked her like a baby in its mother's arms also threatened to unseat her, forcing her to brace herself to keep upright.

The cart was like her life. It was a blessing one moment and shook her to the core the next.

Berwyn and her husband were dressed in Roman togas and wore narrow, linen masks that left their mouths and chins exposed. Stowig sat next to William on the cart's front seat. Matilda was on the side bench in the back, next to Berwyn.

Both she and her cousin wore haceles, the ankle-length, hooded cloak adopted by the Christian monks. The voluminous cloak hid the figure underneath and its hood blocked the face. A hemp cord cinched the cloak at the waist. Long, flowing sleeves covered the hands past the fingertips—making it a mystery whether the wearer was a woman or a man.

The late afternoon sun felt good on her face, but made Matilda hot under the haceles. Though uncomfortable now, after sunset she would appreciate the cloak's warmth.

This would be her last chance to be near Geoff. Deep in thought, she'd been silent for most of the journey. When she looked up, one of the elders caught her eye and questioned her about being so quiet. She said the first thing that came into her head.

"I'm not feeling well."

"How terrible for you, my dear," the wife of the head elder of the woten said. "And on such an occasion."

"Is a little blessing on its way?" the other wife asked.

Matilda blushed. It hadn't dawned on her that people would think her pregnant.

"It feels more like congestion," she lied. "I'll close my eyes and rest until we get there."

Allowed her cocoon of silence, Matilda filtered out the voices swirling around her and listened to the measured *clop-clop* of the ox and the squeaks of the swaying cart. When they neared the manor, she pulled the monk's hood over her hair and down to cover her face.

"Matilda!" Berwyn sounded exasperated. "We can't see you."

"That's the idea. This hood is my mask. William, put yours up too."

During the cart ride, William had told everyone that he and Matilda were staying well away from Lady Rosamund because of her animosity toward his wife. They knew of the troubles in the marketplace and understood.

Matilda's breath constricted and her stomach tied itself in knots as she alighted with trepidation onto the soil of the manor. She followed her cousin to the goat-mowed lawns.

There was no receiving line—since the purpose of a masquerade was to stay unknown—so she and William said their farewells to the elders, who would sit in places of honor near the baron. Matilda led her cousin to a remote table, with

Stowig and Berwyn following. Sprightly music from wandering minstrels lifted her spirits. The knots in her stomach loosened by the time they sat at an empty table on the outskirts of the festivities.

"I cannot believe all this food," Berwyn exclaimed.

The drape of her toga accentuated the sweep of her arm as she gestured toward the retainers conveying steaming bowls of venison stew in a dark broth from the kitchen. On the heels of the stew arrived savory mutton pies, vegetable pies with thick crusts and freshly baked trenchers.

"Upon my oath, this is better than last year," the blacksmith said as he slipped onto the bench next to his wife. "They must have been cooking and baking for days."

Matilda breathed in, savoring the drifting aromas.

William seated himself on the bench, pushing his hood off as he did so and breathing a sigh of relief to be unencumbered.

"What a variety of costumes!" Berwyn said as she started filling the halved trenchers of freshly baked, hard-crusted bread from nearby bowls.

Matilda saw no sign of the satyr, but her eyes took in a Druid priestess, several shepherds with staffs, a few more monks and Romans, a number of colorfully clothed minstrels, a Father Death carrying a cow's skull and even a few dressed in the costume of the hated Vikings.

"Let's eat." Stowig reached for a platter of meat. "No need to wait on the nobility. There are no formalities at a masquerade."

He'd already started in on the food, his broad shoulders hunched as he concentrated on every last morsel.

Exquisite flavors crossed Matilda's taste buds as she put a forkful of rabbit into her mouth. Before she left for Wroxton, she'd have to ask Dunavik what she used to tenderize the meat.

When she cooked a rabbit, it got tough and stringy.

"May we join you?"

Matilda looked up into the eyes of Oslad the baker. With him were his wife, Gwenver, and their almost-grown children, who looked ill at ease.

"Help yourselves," William said, offering them seats without being overly generous in his greeting.

Oslad sat down across the table from William and next to Stowig, placing Matilda out of harm's way and shielding Berwyn as well. Gwenver sat by his side. Their raw-boned, gangly children settled in on the bench next to her cousin. Matilda glanced at Gwenver's dour face, which many said was a direct result of her husband's roving eye. She pointedly complimented the woman on her skillfully sewn gypsy costume and received a broad smile for her efforts.

Matilda was surprised that Gwenver's best friend was not with them.

"Where is Paela?"

"She and Zelif are coming later. He was in bad temper and Paela decided to wait, rather than tempt his ire by coming alone."

Gwenver shook her head slowly as if the grizzled hair on it were a heavy burden.

"That man gives her nothing but trouble. That's what she gets for marrying the most handsome man around. He's too in love with himself to be a good husband."

"Hey!" Oslad protested. "I was as handsome as Zelif when we were young."

He puffed up as he said this, seeming to grow with his conceit.

"Precisely my point," Gwenver responded bitterly, using his

words to confirm hers.

"Would you look at the quality of this bread!" Oslad exclaimed as he reached for a trencher. "I swear the manor kitchens rival my bakery."

"That's saying something," Matilda said with honesty. "You're a great baker."

"Thank you, charming woman."

He looked recovered from his wife's barbs. The young people were relaxed and chattering excitedly.

"Muran is the better musician," one was saying.

"He can't hold a candle to Marisha," the other responded. "She's great. And she can also sing."

Some villagers were dancing, but most were still eating. Food that had been plentiful was now in short supply. Daytime birds extinguished their songs as the earth gave way to the night. A dark-skinned gypsy in native costume worked the tables. Matilda remembered her fortune at the fair. As foretold, she'd had to make tough choices.

Carnulf strolled up, a swarm of children circling around him. The satyr costume created a flurry of interest. His dark curls hid the leather straps that held goat horns to his head. Sheepskin was tied to his legs. He'd painted cloven hooves onto cloth sacks and tied these over his shoes. He looked the embodiment of an ancient satyr. His muscular torso, developed by carrying heavy iron from the forge, was bared to the evening air. Around his neck hung a set of wooden pipes. The overall effect in the early evening dusk was of a wild and ancient god come to earth to carouse energetically.

Without asking, he squeezed in next to Matilda, while shooing the children away. His eyes flashed with excitement in the flickering light of the bonfires.

"The baron must have spent a lot tonight—though he can afford it."

Paela and Zelif arrived and Matilda greeted her enthusiastically. She'd gotten used to Paela's dry, ironic speech and was no longer offended by it.

Zelif remained aloof, avoiding eye contact.

"Rumor has it," Paela said as soon as she was seated, "that Lady Rosamund has a smug smile on her face and everyone is wondering what she's up to."

Gwenver's face lit up with interest, but Matilda's stomach threatened to tie itself into a knot again.

"You missed the best of the food," Gwenver said to Paela. "Perhaps they still have hot food in the kitchens."

"No need to fuss."

Zelif dug in with gusto, his back turned away from the others, making no contribution to the conversation.

More and more couples were drifting to the dancing lawn near a stand of trees. Matilda quickly finished her honey cake so William could escort her out to their first dance of the evening.

"Join us."

Gwenver automatically included Paela by a wave of her arm.

"We'll wait here."

"Too soon for me," Stowig said, patting his stomach as if a physical manifestation was needed to convince anyone of his over-indulgence. His wife looked disappointed.

"Want to dance, Berwyn?" Carnulf asked, reaching for her hand.

"That'll be fun! A Roman matron cavorting with a pagan satyr."

William led them to a far corner where a circle was forming in the light of the bonfires.

The music played in a slow beat. Costumes swished around them, adding their own sounds. Joining hands, they synchronized their steps to the patterns and music. A momentary sadness washed through her. This might be the last chance to dance with her cousin. They may never again see each other after her return to Wroxton. At least, he'd be free to pursue a friendship with Dunavik.

They changed partners and Carnulf joined her for an energetic country dance. His antics matched the free spirit of his fierce satyr costume. Where others took one step, Carnulf threw in several. At the same time, he kept up a line of patter about the music and the dance and the costumes. With the apprentice finding the exact clever word to highlight a folly or exploit an exaggeration, Matilda was soon freely laughing.

"I love when you laugh," he said.

"You seem to find the right words to bring on laughter."

"Given the chance, I would make you laugh forever."

William tapped her on the shoulder and declared himself out of breath.

"I'll rest at the banquet table and watch you from there."

"It'll be difficult keeping an eye on me," she teased her cousin as he and Berwyn headed back to the table. "There are so many haceles borrowed for this masquerade, the monks in the monasteries must be cold tonight."

As she and the satyr joined the dance circle, matching their steps to the tune, Matilda wondered when—or if—Geoff would come to claim his dance.

Much later, Carnulf said he was thirsty and would bring ale from the banquet tables. He pointed to a shadowed elm near a dark stand of trees.

"Wait for me under that tree."

She watched him disappear into the crowd of dancers.

The ancient elm grew beyond the flickering light of the bonfires. She leaned against its trunk, finding the shadows restful.

She was watching the dancers dreamily when a rough hand clamped tightly over her mouth. Panic increased her heartbeat. She struggled to bite the hand and scream.

A sharp blow exploded her head into a burst of brilliant particles of light. Darkness descended.

Chapter Twenty-Eight

The others had drifted off long ago, leaving William alone at the banquet table. He hadn't seen his cousin for some time, though he hadn't worried, knowing she was with Carnulf. Now, here was the satyr, approaching with two drinks in hand and no Matilda. His goat horns were slightly askew. William felt a stab of alarm. He rose from the bench.

"Where's Matilda?"

"I was about to ask you that," Carnulf said.

"I haven't seen her for hours."

"She was waiting for me to bring this drink." Carnulf indicated the mug of ale he was setting on the table. "She said she'd wait under an elm tree. I stood talking with friends and was late getting back. When I returned, she wasn't there."

William had a nagging fear that she might have gotten entangled with the baron or his sister, but he said, "Perhaps she got tired of waiting."

"Must be."

Carnulf slumped onto the bench.

"I'll wait with you. She'll come back here eventually."

"I'll see if I can spot her."

William climbed onto the table. Eyes straining in the darkness, he searched the crowd.

"That looks like Matilda."

He pointed in the direction from which Carnulf had come.

"Her hair is covered, so I can't be sure. But it's a woman's gait, and she's the right height."

He climbed down, putting his hand on the satyr's shoulder for balance.

"Come. We'll look for her together."

The ale abandoned on the table, he and the apprentice made their way through the circling dancers, but arrived too late. No monk's cloak was in sight.

"I don't see her," Williams said. A note of anxiety crept in, straining his voice. "She moved from where I last saw her."

Carnulf stomped a cloven hoof.

"I should've insisted she come with me."

William shook his head.

"You would've had a hard time convincing her to do anything she didn't want to do. But she's sensible. She can take care of herself."

William spoke confidently while failing to convince himself. The baron and his sister had the power to bring about any end they desired—no matter what he or Matilda said about it.

He pointed to the darker, outlying area.

"Let's separate. You go that way."

"Fine. I'll circle round and meet you at the table."

The youth left without waiting for a response.

Ignoring courtesies, William plunged into the midst of the dancers, searching for black, hooded cloaks.

"I'm looking for my wife, Matilda," he anxiously explained time and time again. "She's wearing a cloak like yours. Have you seen her?"

His alarm built with each defeat.

Finally, one person said, "I saw a woman wearing one of those. She was walking that way."

William angled to the left as directed, elbowing his way with apologies, but not allowing indignation to stop him. Matilda was walking toward the head table. He hurried his pace to keep her from disaster. She must avoid another clash of wills with Lady Rosamund.

At last he saw her. He ran up to her before she could disappear again.

"Matilda!" he cried as he grabbed her arm.

The figure turned abruptly, causing the hood to fall backward. It was Keridwen.

"Lost your wife?" she smirked. "You'll need to keep looking."

William watched helplessly as she contemptuously turned her back and strolled slowly away. He'd have to begin again.

The task was formidable because shifting dance patterns caused the robed figures to reappear in different locations. He seemed to have looked at each of them many times over.

Tension built at the back of his neck as he slowly began to fear the worst. Did his cousin change her mind and decide to become Lord Geoff's mistress instead of returning to Wroxton?

The very thought made William's stomach turn over—but he had to know the truth. He headed toward the banquet table to see if she'd returned. If she hadn't, he'd confront the baron.

"Any success?" Carnulf asked him as he hurried up to the table, running his fingers through his hair and disturbing the horns once again. William was taking a brief, but much-needed rest on the bench. He'd become aware of the erratic pounding of his heart. If he didn't watch out, he'd have an attack.

"I thought I'd spotted her, but it was Keridwen in the monk's robe."

"Strange," said Gwenver, who had returned to the table without her husband and children, but with her friend. "Keridwen was in a shepherd's robe earlier this evening. Why would she change?"

William feared foul play.

"Maybe she and Matilda switched costumes to play a joke on me," Carnulf said.

"I can't see Matilda coming up with that," Paela said. "If they switched, it was that devious Keridwen who put her up to it."

"I think you should ask that woman where she got that cloak," Gwenver said.

William rose from the bench, glad for a reprieve from a confrontation with Lord Geoff. Carnulf joined him.

Shoulder to shoulder, they pushed through the throng until they found Keridwen. William gripped her arm.

"Where did you get that cloak?"

Fear briefly widened her eyes before she answered.

"Why do you care?"

"Matilda was wearing a cloak like this," William said. "You were seen wearing a shepherd's costume."

Keridwen's cocky confidence returned.

"I found it. It was under a tree near those woods."

She pointed to the edge of the forest where the large elm grew.

"I was feeling cold, so I put it on. If it's her cloak, you can have it."

"It must be hers," Carnulf said.

She started stripping it off. Underneath, she still wore the shepherd's garment.

"Here. Take it."

She thrust the cloak at William, who hadn't released his grip. The cloak hung loosely on her captured arm, dragging in the dirt.

As he turned to talk with Carnulf, William felt a cold chill.

"Matilda wouldn't willingly take off her cloak," he said. "She wore undergarments beneath. Either it's not her cloak or she's in trouble."

Keridwen, hands on hips, spat out words dripping with venom.

"She's been running after the baron since she first came here. Maybe he gave her something prettier to parade around in."

"Watch your mouth," Carnulf said.

William released his grip on her arm and she staggered backwards.

"Leave the cloak. Get out of my sight."

She quickly disappeared into the nearby crowd.

His reluctance to confront the baron was fast disappearing.

"Keridwen had a good idea. Let's see if the baron has seen Matilda."

By the time he reached the baron's table, William's anger had escalated. He'd demand Matilda's release if the baron had persuaded her to be his mistress. She was too young to understand the consequences.

Despite his ingrained training of obedience, he immediately confronted his lord.

"Where is my wife? You were to keep your hands off her."

The baron sprang up from his seat, knocking his heavy chair to the ground, alarm spreading across his face. Guests seated at the table looked shocked, then interested. Lady Rosamund, who was costumed as a queen, looked smug.

"We haven't seen her."

The baron took the focus off himself by adding the others into his reply. William flushed, realizing how rudely he'd spoken.

"None of us has been away from this table," the baron said, stress evident in his voice. "She hasn't come here."

William heard the ring of truth. His anger died quickly.

"Come," Lord Geoff said as he drew William away from the table, but gestured to Carnulf to stay behind. "Let's step to the side."

When they were out of earshot, the baron took control.

"When did she go missing?"

"About an hour ago. Carnulf came to me. He and Matilda had been dancing. He left to get some mugs of ale. She was missing when he returned to the dancing lawn. He looked for her before coming to me. Then we looked together—to no avail."

The baron's brow furrowed as he glanced Carnulf's way. Clearly, he wasn't pleased that a young rival, bare-chested despite descending cold, had been dancing the night away with Matilda.

"What was she wearing?"

"A monk's cloak. Like mine."

"That makes finding things more difficult. There are so many of those cloaks tonight."

"I fear the worst, I believe we found her cloak and she only wore undergarments beneath it. I thought you might have given her a better cloak to keep her warm."

"Hell's fury." The baron's voice was charged with indignation. "I wouldn't shame her like that."

The light from the bonfires glinted off the metallic links of Lord Geoff's armored costume. He'd shed the bulky helmet, which completed this warrior gear. He pointed to Carnulf, who'd been waiting, shifting from leg to leg, his horns again upright.

"Let's see what he has to say."

"Carnulf!" William shouted and waved to him to come over. He hurried to the baron and repeated his story.

"We'll look again by the elm tree and the table," the baron said. "We have to eliminate those possibilities before I widen the search."

Lord Geoff strode toward his table, saying, "I want to tell my guests why I'm leaving and make sure they keep quiet. There's no need for this to become grist for the gossip mill if she returns on her own."

Told they courted disfavor if word about Matilda leaked out, his guests rapidly agreed to stay silent. Lady Rosamund bristled at the suggestion she would deign to gossip.

"She is far beneath me. I take no notice of such people."

The three men started on their quest. Only the flickering bonfires kept the darkness at bay. A chilling cold seeped stealthily into William's bones and he began to shiver—whether brought on by the night air or his fears for Matilda, he couldn't say.

Matilda slowly regained consciousness. With it came terror. Her hands were bound, her stomach was nauseated and her head pounded from the jerky movements of the horse. Horse? She was draped over a saddle, with the rough, smelly leggings of the rider pressed against her nose. She twisted, trying to drop to the ground.

"Hey, you. Stop that." she heard a gruff male voice say. The horse pranced excitedly as she received a solid blow to the head and lost consciousness.

Chapter Twenty-Nine

In phalanx formation, the men descended on the elm, the dancers parting before them as they saw the baron approaching. Matilda wasn't there. William's heart sank. It had been almost two hours since she was last seen. A glance at Lord Geoff showed he shared the disappointment.

The baron scoured the earth around the tree, moving objects with his foot to determine their identity, picking up others for closer inspection as if to find some evidence of Matilda. Seemingly satisfied there was nothing to find, he said, "We'll try the banquet table. You lead the way, William."

Silently, they skirted the edge of the crowd, keeping a steady pace. As they approached the table, he saw that Stowig and Berwyn had returned and put cloaks over their Roman togas in deference to the cold.

"Have you seen my wife?"

"No. We assumed you two were dancing."

Stowig glanced at the baron, looking curious.

"Matilda was with Carnulf when she went missing. Lord Geoff is helping us search."

"We'll help," Berwyn said. "Going off without a word is unlike her."

William could think of a few times when this wasn't true,

but he'd forgive those times just to have his cousin reappear.

Working adeptly, Lord Geoff quickly divided the lawn area into search quadrants, choosing boundaries with objects easily identifiable in the darkness.

"Each of us will go in a different direction and return here in a half hour with or without William's wife. If we haven't found her by then, we'll stop the dancing and form search parties to scour the woods and the village. We'll use dogs if need be."

"You there!" he shouted to a passing retainer. "Bring us torches at once!"

The servant jumped to obey his formidable master. In the flickering light of the huge bonfires, the meshed-maille links in the baron's armor threw flashes into the darkness. He stood solidly affixed to the earth by thick leather riding boots. The warm, royal blue tunic beneath this chest-protecting webbing met the top of his riding boots at the knee and covered his arms down to the wrist, shielding their master from the evening chill.

William watched Carnulf remove his goat horns and don a heavy, sleeved tunic to protect against the cold. The woolen wraps stayed strapped to his legs, but he took off the painted-rag hooves. The satyr was disappearing and a hot-blooded youth taking its place.

Berwyn and Stowig stood by attentively.

The baron assigned a quadrant to each of them.

"I'll search the path to the village close to where she was last seen. She may have started down it, fallen and can't be heard above all this noise."

Impatient to get on with it, William walked rapidly toward his quadrant. He understood the baron's strategy to delay raising an alarm, but his instincts said it was wrong. His instincts wanted an immediate, full-fledged investigation.

Diligently, he scoured his quadrant with negative results, turning progressively more dour with each setback. As he returned to the rendezvous point, a great tiredness weighed on him. He saw the baron sitting alone at the table, a lit torch spiked into the yielding soil beside him.

"No sign of her," Lord Geoff said, looking more troubled as William drew near, "and I walked a third of the path." The baron tapped his foot, a frown creasing his forehead. "After the others report in and if Matilda isn't found, I'll send people all the way down to your cottage."

"I'm worried. I believe her cloak is the one we took from Keridwen. If true, something bad as happened. She wouldn't stand around in the night air in undergarments."

"I wouldn't put it past Keridwen to be pointing us in the wrong direction," the baron said, his face echoing the anxiety William felt.

William wrung his hands. He decided to be candid with his lord, although he'd hold his tongue about the false marriage. Matilda must have had reasons for not revealing she was free.

"When I first found her missing, I worried you or your sister had her. I've seen her eyes when she looks on you. Her feelings run deep. I feared you'd found a way to persuade her to become your mistress."

Music and merriment melted into background. Night sounds hushed as if nature herself were listening.

"I can't deny I love her."

William could feel the pain behind the words.

"It's because I love her that I let her go. I respect her wishes."

Before the baron could say anything more, Carnulf emerged from the crowd and reported in.

"She's nowhere to be seen."

Some revelers, curious, looked their way, but most stayed involved in their own enjoyment. Noisy, lively music and laughter intruded on the solemnity of the search, irritating William.

The baron rose.

"Go to the manor. Ask Dunavik to organize a search of all the rooms, including the cellars."

The apprentice nodded.

"Tell Dunavik to report to me at the head table. When done, return there and bring more torches."

Carnulf departed, greeting a tired looking Stowig and Berwyn as they passed. They reported negative results.

"Choose someone to go with you to search the path to William's cottage," the baron instructed Stowig. "Take torches and look for signs of a struggle or of someone entering the woods. Watch for anything dropped or caught on branches."

The baron raised his voice over the music. "Check the cottage, the barn and the grounds. Return using the same trail. Sometimes things look different from the opposite direction, especially at night. Listen carefully. She may be injured and trying to call out."

Stowig nodded agreement, and the baron turned to Berwyn.

"Take three people with you. Scour the roadway, with two of you checking the sides and two walking the middle. If you find nothing, have the others check cottage-by-cottage while you return by the road. I'll either be at the head table or I'll have left word where to find me."

William watched Berwyn and Stowig pick up torches and leave to find more searchers.

The baron grabbed an armful of torches. "William, come with me and bring the rest of these. We're going to need them tonight."

They skirted the fringe of the dancing lawn where clowns cavorted with shepherdesses, patrician ladies circled in the arms of farmers, and nuns joined hands with bandits. The bizarre scene, with squeals and shouts breaking through the laughter, caused William's head to pound.

As he and the baron strode up to the head table where Lady Rosamund and her party lounged lazily, Carnulf arrived, out of breath.

"Those I talked with in the manor haven't seen Matilda. Nor is anyone there who is not supposed to be there. Dunavik is organizing a search."

The baron nodded, then gripped the young man's forearm.

"Stay here to wait for Stowig and Berwyn. They're searching the path and roadway. Also, have someone bring my hunting dogs to you."

"Yes, my lord!" Carnulf said eagerly.

"William and I are going to halt the dancing and question the dancers. I'll need you to organize the volunteers I select from among them into search parties and to keep me informed as they report in."

"You can count on me."

"I'm bored," the baron's sister announced, rising from her chair. "I'm going to bed." She yawned dramatically. "I can't understand why you're making a fuss."

She departed, taking her entourage of friends with her.

William's neck bristled, but he held his tongue despite the provocation from Lady Rosamund as he and Lord Geoff approached the musicians.

"Stop playing," the baron shouted.

The abrupt halt to the music caused everyone to mill around. The baron climbed onto a nearby table to speak.

"William's wife, Matilda, is missing."

His words hung in the night air.

"She's wearing a monk's robe. Step forward if you've seen her lately."

Muttering broke out as people grappled with the seriousness of the interruption of their pleasures. No one stepped forward.

"We need volunteers to scour the lawn and the edges of the forest."

A general shuffling rippled through the strange gathering, made grotesque by the flickering light of the bonfires. William found the demons, soldiers and deities emerging from the crowd unsettling.

"One more thing," the baron shouted, "we're looking for Keridwen. If you see her, bring her to me."

He jumped down from the bench.

William and Lord Geoff questioned the dancers who stepped forward. Some had seen Matilda earlier in the evening, but no one knew where she was now. Sleepy children stirred in parents' arms and the baron sent them home.

Villagers were spreading across the lawn with torches. Weird patterns of light and shadow distorted costumed Romans, Danes, pagan priestesses and blue-painted Celts as they roamed the grounds. Dogs raced back and forth, yelping excitedly as if taking part in some new gaiety planned for the evening.

Two men burst from the crowd, holding a struggling

Keridwen, still dressed in her shepherdess frock, but with a shawl covering her shoulders against the cold. The baron gestured for William to come with him and told the others to wait.

Lord Geoff drew the woman aside, away from the curious. He held her arm tightly so she couldn't escape.

"Why do you treat me like this?" she cried out. "I'm a favorite of your lady sister. I do her bidding."

"My sister can't protect you if I find out you're involved in Matilda's disappearance."

"I told all I know. I found the cloak under the elm tree."

She replied defiantly, her stance cocky and assured. William believed she must be more afraid of Lady Rosamund than the baron.

"Who was near you to confirm your story?"

"I don't know. They were all in costumes. It was dark."

The baron shook her.

"You're known to be jealous of Matilda. You had her cloak. What did you do with her?"

Her eyes widened as she twisted in his grip, but she stayed silent.

Lord Geoff turned to the two men who had delivered Keridwen.

"Take her to the dungeon. When she decides she wants to talk, bring her to me."

Keridwen was dragged off, screeching her innocence.

"It's not me you want. I didn't take her away."

"I know she's hiding something," the baron said, his brow furrowed in a deep frown. "I wish I knew what. With each delay, Matilda is in greater danger—if only from the cold."

Stowig returned.

"We didn't find her. We searched the obvious places."

William's heart plummeted.

"We need dogs for anything more."

The baron agreed.

"Follow me. We'll check on the arrival of the dogs."

William, Stowig and several others trailed after the baron. The clinking of armor matched the beat of the baron's rapid pace.

"I want to search the woods," William said to him as they hurried toward Carnulf. "I feel useless standing around."

"Stay with me. News will get back to me first. It's better you're here when she returns."

The baron was right, although it didn't make him feel any better.

"We need a piece of her clothing," Lord Geoff said. "I should've told Stowig to bring something."

Paela, walking closely behind, said, "I'll get it. I feel badly for dear Matilda. I'd like to help."

Lord Geoff turned slightly in her direction.

"Agreed." He then added.

"William, where's the clothing Matilda wore last? It'll carry the most scent."

"What about the cloak?"

"We don't know for sure it's hers. I don't want to send the dogs off on a wrong scent."

William nodded.

"She wore the brown linen hanging on the hook near the bed."

Paela left for the cottage.

They arrived at the head table to learn that the dogs were being rounded up and would be ready within the half hour. Stowig sat down to wait for them. William noticed Carnulf was showing considerable organizational skill—deploying volunteers and giving clear, concise reports.

Villagers who had searched the banquet area returned to report no sign of Matilda. Berwyn returned from the village. Every home, barn and shelter had been searched. No Matilda.

William felt shaken and exhausted. The baron looked more frantic with each negative report.

Chapter Thirty

Three hours had passed since Matilda went missing. William watched the musicians pack up their instruments. Servants removed leftover food and carried tables and chairs into the manor. The baron clapped him on the shoulder to draw him to one side.

Speaking quietly, as if not wanting to be overheard, Lord Geoff confessed, "I feel responsible. I fear it's because I interfered in your lives that Matilda is missing."

"I should've kept a closer eye on her," William said, disheartedly.

"If she was deliberately harmed, I swear I'll kill the man who harmed her."

"Be careful what you swear," William cautioned, alarmed at the baron's intensity. "Your sister may be involved in this." He felt embarrassed to have spoken so bluntly.

Lord Geoff assumed a defensive stance, as if to shield his family's honor.

"That cannot be. Rosamund was with me all evening and had little interest in talking with anyone but her personal friends."

He took a seat and William sat next to him.

"I envy you your wife." The baron spoke quietly.

"I've been fortunate to have two extraordinary women in my life."

"I was young when your first wife died," the baron reminisced, "but I remember how kind she was to me."

William felt aglow at the memory.

"Aelswitha was love at first sight. Once I saw her, I couldn't rest until she was mine."

The baron wrung his hands.

"Matilda affected me the same, but how do you know true love from a passing fancy?"

It was an articulation of the baron's extreme anxiety that he'd even ask. Concern broke down social barriers and taboos.

"There are ways to know. With Aelswitha, she filled my every thought from when I awoke in the morning until I slept, and then she shared my dreams."

"Whenever I think of Matilda," the baron said, "I want to fold her in my arms so tightly we become one."

"With Aelswitha, I could finish her sentence and she could finish mine."

"Even while I argue with Matilda, I love her."

"While I was at work or when I was with friends, each brief thought of Aelswitha brought a smile."

"One fleeting glimpse of Matilda and the cock awakes."

"I dragged Aelswitha from danger, never thinking of myself."

The baron's troubled voice broke.

"But for my foolish pride—if Matilda had been free—I would've married her against all protests."

William was taken aback. Lord Geoff was deeply in love.

"I recognize in you the depth of love I had for my Aelswitha.

If you had proposed marriage, I wouldn't have stood in the way. Our marriage was a pretense to protect her from Sir Loric."

The baron looked shaken.

When he found his voice, he bared his soul.

"Matilda once asked if I'd marry her. I told her I had to marry a Norman noblewoman."

"That's probably why she never revealed her secret."

Dunavik bustled up to them. William felt embarrassed. She'd almost caught them speaking about personal matters.

"Matilda isn't in the manor," the chatelaine reported. "I don't think she ever was there tonight."

She stated this with certainty.

"I personally checked the ground floor and bedchambers and had the attics and the cellars searched. Lady Rosamund and her guests are in their chambers. They didn't see anything."

The baron turned to William.

"Your suggestion that my sister could be involved is unthinkable. It has to be Keridwen."

"That one's into petty stuff," Dunavik countered, "but she lacks the imagination for something serious."

"We're waiting for the dogs and a piece of Matilda's clothing to start tracking her."

"Oh, that dear child," Dunavik exclaimed. "I hope you're wrong about someone deliberately wanting to harm her."

She turned to William.

"And you, poor man. Is there anything I can do for you?"

William shook his head.

"Well, I'll make sure she's well taken care of when she's

safely returned."

Dunavik left for the manor saying she'd fetch warm blankets and have hot food ready. Lord Geoff and William resumed their seats. Night sounds penetrated as they sat, waiting.

Chapter Thirty-One

"We have to assume foul play, William," Lord Geoff said to him as they sat at the head table discussing Matilda's disappearance. "She wouldn't have deliberately hidden herself, and..."

He was interrupted by two men dragging a reluctant Keridwen.

"Take your hands off me!" she shouted, struggling to free herself.

Keridwen may have told her captors she was ready to talk, but now that she was out of the cell she'd returned to her own obstructive nature.

"Not until you tell the truth," Lord Geoff said as William looked on.

The woman answered warily. "Lady Rosamund gave me instructions to put the cloak over my costume and walk around for awhile. She instructed me how to answer if questioned."

The baron loomed over the servant.

"Lies. My sister never left our table."

Keridwen cringed, pulling back from him.

"She sent her instructions with a man."

"No man came to our table to talk with my sister," the baron said adamantly.

She was becoming increasingly subdued, seeming to realize she was caught up in something bigger than she first understood.

"I do what my lady tells me. I don't ask questions."

"Why would my sister send such instructions to you?"

"I don't know why. I just obey."

William decided Keridwen's head must be spinning from the pressure of questions.

"Who was the man?"

"It was strange. The man was one of her horse attendants, not a manor servant."

"Which one?"

"I don't know his name. A big man, with dark hair, strong."

"If I send you to the stables with these men, can you pick him out?"

"Why not just ask your sister?" William said, breaking into the conversation. In normal circumstances, he would never do this.

"Lady Rosamund is abed already. I don't want to disturb her," Geoff replied gruffly.

"I'd recognize him," Keridwen said.

"If he isn't in the stables, ask around. When you find him, bring him to me."

Keridwen and the two men hurried off.

Paela returned with the dress, just as the hunting dogs arrived, barking and straining at their leashes. The baron instructed Carnulf to go with the dog handlers to the elm. The handlers would give the dogs the scent from Matilda's dress.

William listened to the yelping of the dogs fade as the entourage moved farther and farther away. He longed to be with them. He felt so useless waiting. Two horses stood saddled, awaiting them when needed.

Keridwen returned with her two guards.

"I couldn't find the stable hand. I'm told his friend is one of the searchers. Maybe he knows where to find him."

"Locate this friend and send the man to me."

Keridwen and her two caretakers left as hoof beats rattled the earth. Riders had been sent into the village so that news could be relayed quickly.

"No news yet. We're probing haystacks and the creek."

William's shoulders slumped. They were looking for a body.

After a few more rapid-fire questions by the baron, the man rode off to the village. Lord Geoff and he were again alone.

"If she's dead," the baron cried out, "I'll kill the one responsible with my bare hands."

William forced his voice to sound reassuring.

"She can't be dead. We'll find her."

Keridwen returned with Paela's husband. Zelif's costume was disheveled and he looked frightened.

"Do you know where the monk's robe came from that Keridwen was given to wear tonight?"

"I had nothing to do with this kidnapping."

Lord Geoff's eyes flared.

"Kidnapping?"

Zelif cowered.

"I overheard your sister speaking to her stablehand."

He spoke rapidly as if needing to get this off his chest.

"I didn't know they were serious. I don't know where they put her. If I knew, I would've said. I've been searching, trying to find her."

"What did you overhear?" Lord Geoff's voice cut to the bone.

"Your lady sister said Matilda was a thorn in her side. She wanted to get rid of her once and for all."

"What!"

"They seemed to know what kind of costume she'd be wearing. Lady Rosamund said she'd have some of her friends wear the same costume to confuse things."

"I thought it was unusual to see so many monks," Lord Geoff said through gritted teeth.

"What else did you hear?" William asked anxiously.

Zelif paused as if to stay silent, but changed his mind after a glance at the baron. "Lady Rosamund said Edrich knew what to do and he'd be paid well. I didn't know they meant kidnapping."

The baron looked fiercely grim.

"Where is this man now?"

"I don't know. I haven't seen him since." Zelif was sweating under the pressure, despite the chill of the evening.

Paela ran to her husband and pummelled him.

"How could you harm that dear woman?"

"It wasn't serious," he protested. "A joke, we were told. She was to be rescued later tonight."

Lord Geoff instructed men nearby. "Have Carnulf hold him and Keridwen under arrest until I get this sorted out. William, we'll go to my sister."

Geoff was fuming as he barged through the massive front door and took the broad staircase two steps at a time. Dunavik joined them as they reached his sister's bedchamber.

Not knocking, he burst in, slamming the chamber door against the wall. Already abed, Rosamund bolted upright and screamed, "Get out of here!"

"Not until you tell me where Matilda is."

"I wouldn't know."

Her nose pinched as if she smelled a bad odor.

"Why do you search for that peasant? Remember your place in society."

Geoff strode to the bed and grabbed his sister by the shoulders. "Where's Matilda?"

"How would I know?" Rosamund gasped defiantly.

Enraged by her defiance, he threw her back onto the pillows.

"You were overheard plotting against her."

Rosamund's eyebrows shot upward, but she still managed a haughty tone.

"If I was overheard, then it was also overheard that I don't know exactly where she was taken."

"What do you mean?"

"I left it to my man to decide what to do with her."

"You were overheard saying 'You know your orders'. What were those orders?"

He stared fiercely at his sister.

Rosamund shrugged casually as if anything she chose to do was all right if it pertained to one of the lower classes.

"I told him to dump her in one of your hunting sheds far enough away that she wouldn't be easily found. I've arranged to move her out of the shire. If you'll not protect your noble name, then I'll protect it for you."

He uttered a strangled cry and gripped his sister by the

throat. Her skin turned white, then red.

"You'll tell me where she is."

Rosamund tore at his hands. Unable to break his hold, she hissed, "I told you I don't know. Only Edrich knows."

"Where's Edrich?"

Geoff released his grip, and Rosamund fell back against the silken coverlet, massaging her throat and glaring at her brother.

"I don't know," she said hoarsely. "He was to return here for the other half of his payment, but he hasn't."

"What does he look like?" William demanded urgently.

Rosamund seemed to focus on the others in the room.

"Get out of here. All of you."

"You'll reply or take the consequences," Geoff threatened, his blood boiling.

She must have seen something in his look. "Above average height. Very muscular. Dark hair cut evenly all around. His nose has been smashed in a fight. He was wearing a brown tunic and leggings when I saw him this afternoon. I don't know what he wore to the masquerade." She paused, wrinkling her nose, and then added, "He tends to smell of horses and manure."

He turned to Dunavik. "Do you know this man?"

"Yes."

"Is this an accurate description?"

"It is."

"Get Edrich's description to every searcher," he instructed her. "Have him brought to me as soon as he's found."

He turned back to Rosamund when Dunavik left the chamber.

"Be out of here within the hour."

His sister's mouth opened, aghast, and her eyes widened in shock. She rose from the bed, her manner pleading. She looked deathly pale.

"Geoffrey! You can't mean this."

"You have no conception of what you've done."

"But I'm your sister."

"I won't tolerate you under my roof. Dress and be gone. What you can't pack will be sent after you."

"I'll be on the roads at night. What about bandits?"

"Take your chances in the dark and cold—just as Matilda must. Be prepared for consequences when you hurt the woman I love."

William stepped backwards, looking stunned that he would reveal this aloud.

Rosamund screeched, "Love? You can't love that low-born bitch."

Unable to stomach more from his sister, he backhanded her so that she fell across her silken bed.

"Get out. Now."

Chapter Thirty-Two

Geoff's rage was all consuming and he fought to regain self-control as he strode rapidly toward the head table. The jiggling of his armor added a metallic musical rhythm to the night sounds. A subdued William followed.

Muted voices echoed across the lawn, still plunged in darkness. The earth would soon begin to awaken.

The dogs had returned, their constant movement adding a touch of chaos. Yipping, tails wagging in anticipation, they seemed to be enjoying this unexpected late-night adventure. Jaelyn, the chief tracker, spoke as they approached.

"Matilda's scent was strong by the tree, but little scent remains on the ground going away from the tree. We found signs at the edge of the woods of a tethered horse. We sent a couple of hounds and searchers by foot to follow that horse's trail. The rest of the dogs are here. What do you want us to do?"

"Send someone to the stables and get a piece of Edrich's clothing," the baron directed. "He's behind all this. He must have carried Matilda so the dogs cannot easily find her among all these revelers. We'll use his scent instead."

Geoff turned to William. "We'll ride out with the dogs and leave some volunteers here to forward messages."

As he removed his armor, he studied William.

"Will you be warm enough in that cloak? Do you want riding boots?"

"I could use riding boots, but I'm warm enough."

Geoff ordered a cloak for himself and riding boots for William. The boy took off, running. By the time Geoff had removed his armor, the cloak and boots had arrived.

"My cart and ox are still here," William said, looking concerned. "I should see to them."

Geoff dropped onto the bench beside the woodcutter, who was pulling on sturdy riding boots.

"No, they aren't. Berwyn said her husband took the elders back to the village while we were questioning the dancers. He was to put your ox and cart back into your barn and join the search of the cottages."

"I can depend on my friends to look out for me."

Geoff sprang up from the bench. "Let's mount the horses so we're ready when they return with Edrich's clothing."

At his signal, the saddled horses were brought. His war horse stood stoically, waiting for its cue to move, undistracted by noise, torches and movement. William's horse shifted nervously, whinnying and shaking its head. With long legs and physical strength, the woodcutter soon had the horse under control.

"We'll go to Carnulf," Geoff said. "He hasn't reported in lately."

He left instructions for sending the stablehand's clothing to the tracker before kicking his heels to the sides of his horse.

Chapter Thirty-Three

Pain moved in searing waves up her leg, waking her fully from the blackness that enveloped her. It found its way into her consciousness, bringing with it a premonition of danger.

Matilda opened her eyes, slowly becoming oriented to her surroundings. Nothing looked familiar.

Dense tree cover overhung tangled thicket lining the steep embankment of a creek. She was lying upside down at the bottom of it. Water pulled at her hair, her head throbbed, and her left ankle felt enormously swollen. Moist earth cradled her and cold seeped into her soggy clothing. Swiftly flowing water brushed against her hair. It created a strange, musical backdrop to her awareness of menace. Fear crept in.

"How did I get here?"

She remembered waiting under an ancient elm at the edge of the manor house grounds. Rough hands had grabbed her, lifting her off her feet. Another hand had clamped over her mouth to keep her from crying out. She took a solid blow to the head that even her abundant hair couldn't cushion. She recalled a brief struggle on a horse before awakening here, alone, in the dark.

"I must get home."

Thank the gods, her hands had been untied before she was thrown down the embankment. She rolled onto her side and pushed herself upright, grimacing.

"I hope my ankle bone isn't cracked."

She grabbed a nearby sapling to try to stand, but her injured ankle wouldn't support weight. Pain forced her back onto the wet soil. She must await rescue.

"But who knows I'm missing? And worse, who wants me right here?"

Gingerly, she pressed at the bump on her aching head, deciding there was nothing she could do about it, and then wrung the water from her tangled, mud-matted hair. She shivered violently as the night air chilled her damp body. Her masquerade costume—a voluminous monk's robe—was missing. She'd been left with only her flimsy undergarments for warmth.

"Whoever took my heavy robe probably thinks I'm already dead."

A brisk breeze created goose flesh on her arms. She shivered.

"If I'm out here much longer, they'll be proven right."

She moved dry leaves and pine needles to cushion her hips from dampness and wrapped a length of dry underskirt around her shoulders.

Pain reasserted itself. She fought to keep from slipping back into unconsciousness. Breathing deeply, taking in the aroma of wet vegetation, she willed the blackness to move on.

The masquerade dance on the baron's estate would last until dawn. With so many merrymakers spilling across the manor grounds, the music and laughter should carry long distances on the night air. Yet, she heard nothing.

"I must be well away from the manor grounds."

Shouting would clearly be to no avail.

She heard scurrying sounds. These deep woods were home to boars and packs of wild dogs. Her heart beat rapidly. She stared into the branches along the embankment, but saw nothing.

Groping nearby, she felt a stout, gnarled branch. After testing it for weight and strength, she placed it next to her, releasing a fervent prayer that it would prove hardy enough to keep wild dogs at bay.

She cried out when she heard movement again.

"God help me!"

She grasped the stick with both hands, but there was nothing to be seen and, now, not a thing to be heard. Whatever had moved in the thicket was staying well out of her range of vision.

Matilda felt pulsing aches from the bruising on her outstretched arms. She shivered in the cold. It was already making her sleepy.

"I don't want to die."

She resisted remembering the dilemma that caused her to be cast down this embankment. Her vision blurred with tears as unwanted memories poured in.

"Let me be," she cried out. "I have enough just to stay alive."

She fled gladly into unconsciousness.

Geoff nudged his warhorse slowly forward, staying to the edge of the dancing green. Edrich's clothing must have been found because he heard yapping which meant the dogs were on the move.

The horse rocked him in rhythmic patterns. Mixed in with the muted voices drifting on the night air, the rhythmic squeak of saddle leather had a strangely calming effect. He edged his horse to one side so that he could ride next to William. Since his spontaneous declaration of love, he felt a kinship with the man.

"Why didn't I see Rosamund's hatred?"

"We blind ourselves to the faults of those close to us."

Geoff slumped in the saddle.

"I allowed myself to get caught in my sister's social snobbery. It's meaningless when faced with life or death."

His body twitched with guilt as thoughts flooded in of the night he forced Matilda to relinquish her honor. That one evil had been a potting soil for his sister's hatred.

"I love your cousin to distraction. I fear for my sanity without her. Yet, I know I cannot have her."

"My love for Aelswitha was the same," William said. "When she died, I thought I must die. But I found, as time went on, the pain left."

"Sometimes life only gives us one chance. I pray today I get a second chance to undo the evil I caused."

"If Matilda is alive, she'll survive," William said matter-of-factly. "She knows how to take care of herself."

As they halted their horses near the elm, they heard shouting.

"Here's Edrich!"

In the distant torchlight, Geoff saw a group of men surrounding a horse and rider. One held the bridle. Another had pulled the reins from the rider's hands. Rage mounted as he realized this was the man who kidnapped Matilda.

His heart beat wildly as he galloped to him and leapt to the ground. He pulled the burly man from his horse and punched him squarely in the mouth so that his head snapped back. A trickle of blood appeared at the corner of his lips.

"Where is Matilda?"

The man shook his head as if to clear it and raised his hands to protect his face.

"Mercy."

Geoff took a firmer grip on the rough-woven brown tunic and yanked the man so that he was on tiptoes and eye-to-eye.

"Are you Edrich?"

"I'm Edrich."

"You took a woman into the forest?"

"As ordered by my Lady Rosamund." His brows raised in fear. "I didn't know her name. Only her description and where to find her. I'm going now to see to my lady."

"To collect your money," Geoff said contemptuously. "My sister has been sent away. You deal with me."

He pulled the clothing tighter under Edrich's chin.

"The woman you kidnapped is dear to me. Your life is in peril. Tell me truthfully where you took her. And quickly, if you want to live."

The stable hand stammered in panic. "I-I was only following orders."

Anger rose hotly along Geoff's spine. He released the man who seemed to have trouble standing.

"I want to know exactly what those orders were."

"Zelif and I were to take her from under that elm tree after another man brought her there."

Paela screamed at her husband's villainy. Zelif shrunk into the background, but was prevented from escaping by the villagers.

"I was to put the woman on my horse and leave her at a

forest hunting shed until the other man came for her. I was to leave her cloak under the elm for the shepherdess Kerwiden."

"Who is this other man?" Geoff asked him, rage eating at his gut.

"No one told me a name. He approached me with directions to the hunting shed."

"Where is she?"

"Things didn't work out right," Edrich said, looking frightened.

"What do you mean?"

"She woke. I hit her to keep her quiet and she stopped breathing."

Geoff howled with fury. Edrich cowered.

"I took the rope off her wrists and tried to get her to stand up, but she was dead. I was getting ready to bury her when I heard a creek and dumped her there."

Geoff hurled himself at the kidnapper, his fingers encircling his neck.

"Villain!"

Edrich's face flushed deep red and strangling noises came from his throat as Geoff's thumb pressed ever harder against his Adam's apple.

William grabbed his hands, trying to pry them open. "Don't kill him," he pleaded. "We need this man to show us where Matilda's body is."

Tossing Edrich aside, Geoff yelled, "Carnulf!"

The youth didn't appear.

"He headed down the path to the village some time ago," someone said. "After the dogs were put on the trail."

Angry that Carnulf went missing at this critical time, Geoff turned to the tracker.

"Have Zelif and Keridwen taken to a cell. Bind Edrich to his horse. Organize the dogs and trackers. Bring a suitable horse for the body."

Jaelyn issued orders rapidly and villagers hurried to carry them out. Zelif was dragged off in the direction of the manor, his protests that he was merely following orders ringing loudly, but ineffectively, into the night air.

Edrich climbed willingly onto the horse as if it were a sanctuary from the baron's wrath. A villager gripped the reins so he couldn't flee. His hands were tied in front of him.

Geoff and William remounted. The dogs were brought forward and the volunteers gathered around. Geoff angled his horse toward the woods.

"Jaelyn, ask that piece of scum which direction he took. Track the hoof prints so he doesn't lead us astray."

The baron turned in the saddle. "Torches for the tracker," he yelled.

Several men ran forward, their torches illuminating the tracks of Edrich's horse entering the forest.

Geoff shouted, "Paela, are you here?"

"Right here, my lord," she replied, then began to cry. "I'm so sorry. I had no idea my husband was a part of this."

The baron waved off her apology. "Did you bring a garment of Matilda's?"

"Yes, my lord."

"Give it to Jaelyn for the dogs to smell the scent."

She handed the peplo to the tracker who tied it onto his saddle. Geoff was ready to order the trackers to start the search when William cried out.

"Wait! I want to fetch Matilda's scarlet cloak. I want to wrap her body in something she treasured."

Geoff understood William's need. The enormity of his own loss weighed down on him. He would rein in his impatience long enough for his love to be wrapped in something she cherished.

"Hurry. We won't leave without you."

William turned the horse in the direction of the road and dug his heels into its sides until it was racing across the darkened grounds. I've turned as reckless as the baron, he thought as he quickly traversed the manor grounds and galloped down the road and through the village.

As he dismounted at the cottage, he noticed two horses tied nearby and heard rummaging around inside. He quickened his pace. As he crossed the threshold, he found Carnulf stacking Matilda's clothing and jewelry on the bed. He noticed Matilda's kitten rested on its belly on the chair by the table, its eyes intent on Carnulf and its tail twitching.

"What's going on?"

The apprentice jerked around toward the doorway and glared.

"Stay out of this, William. You don't deserve her."

"What are you talking about?" He was totally bewildered.

Carnulf moved aggressively forward and William stepped backward out of the doorway.

"She's mine, now. Lady Rosamund arranged it. Matilda and I will live on the coast in one of her husband's estates."

"What are you saying? You were helping us—organizing the searches."

"Delaying the searches, you mean. Keeping you out of the woods as long as possible. What luck the baron put me in charge. By dawn I'll have Matilda as my own."

"You bastard!"

William's anger surged as he began to understand Carnulf's treachery. He was glad to turn the traitor's victory to ashes.

"Matilda is dead."

Carnulf looked stunned.

"Dead?"

"Edrich hit her too hard and then dropped her body in a creek."

Carnulf slumped onto the bed.

"But she was to be mine. You're too old for her. She laughs with me."

"She would never have been yours. She loved the baron."

Carnulf looked like he received another great blow.

When William made a move to enter the cottage, the apprentice growled, "Stay where you are, William. You're now the problem." Carnulf drew a blade from his boot.

"But you were our friend."

"Not yours. Only Matilda's."

Carnulf pushed himself off the bed, crossed the room and leapt over the threshold to slash out, cutting into the sleeve of the monk's robe.

William grabbed the long, wooden handle of his woodsman's axe resting alongside the doorframe. With the ease of a lifetime of chopping down trees, he swung the great axe and embedded it in the apprentice's breastbone.

Carnulf looked puzzled as blood bubbled out of his mouth. He grabbed the handle of the axe as he slumped onto his knees and died face downward in the dirt.

"Traitor."

William spit on Carnulf.

Leaving the body where it lay, he rushed inside the cottage, still trembling from the heat of anger coursing through his veins.

He grabbed Matilda's scarlet cloak and wrapped it in a shawl to protect it from the blood staining his clothing. He removed the monk's cloak and put on a heavy tunic. The reality of the last few minutes set in, causing him to shake as he was changing clothes. As he left the cottage, the kitten left with him. It walked to Carnulf's body, sniffed at the blood, then turned her rear end to the apprentice—tail held high—and walked slowly toward the barn.

After tying the bundle to the saddle, William remounted and shortly was at the baron's side.

Chapter Thirty-Four

"What's the matter?" Geoff asked, sensing William's agitation.

"Carnulf was the man your lady sister hired to take Matilda from the hunting shed to to her estate on the coast."

Rage poured through him.

"The bastard. I'll throw him in the dungeon. He'll never see the light of day."

"I killed him with my axe."

Geoff was startled, then immensely relieved. The traitor paid the ultimate sacrifice. He slapped the woodcutter on the back.

"You've become a warrior like me."

With William returned, they could be on their way. He turned to Jaelyn.

"Are we ready?"

"Ready, my lord."

"Lead us out to the creek, Edrich. And no tricks."

The man flinched as if being struck.

Torch in hand, Jaelyn walked slightly ahead to follow the sign where the stable hand's horse had pushed through the underbrush. The gloom of their mission settled on Geoff's shoulders.

"Wouldn't it be faster to use the dogs?"

"I will soon, my lord," Jaelyn said. "It's better to check on Edrich's direction by sight first so we don't get a false trail. Anyway, we can't travel quickly in the dark without risking injury."

Geoff chaffed at the need for caution.

"Edrich, describe this creek," he bellowed.

The kidnapper's voice quivered.

"I didn't really see it. I just followed its noise through the underbrush."

"Idiot."

"Her struggling spooked my horse. It got me turned around so I didn't know the direction any longer. Then I heard the creek and decided to leave her there. The horse found its way back."

"Cur."

The man cringed, as if hunching his shoulders could fend off verbal blows.

"We must get her body before the wild animals get at it," Geoff insisted.

At least, he could do that much for her—even with a black, aching hole where his heart once beat.

Chapter Thirty-Five

In a little over a half hour, they met up with the searchers whose dogs had followed the scent of the horse tethered at the edge of the forest near the elm tree. Coming across this search party relieved Geoff's fear that Edrich was leading them on a wild goose chase.

Berwyn waved a greeting as she approached the baron.

"The dogs lost the scent several times," she reported. "We had to backtrack."

Geoff gestured toward the culprit, who ducked. "At my sister's orders, Edrich abducted her."

"Matilda must be so frightened."

A black shroud dampen his soul. He could barely get the words out.

"She's dead. He killed her. We're trying to find her body."

In the light of the torches, Berwyn looked horrified.

"I'll beat Edrich to a pulp," she declared with venom.

"You'll have to stand in line."

Matilda emerged slowly from the blackness.

She rested, gathering strength, the cool breeze attacking her damp clothing as she listened to the rushing creek and the hoot of a night owl. The mossy earth on which she lay emitted the moisture-laden odor of decaying leaves, rich in its potential to create black earth and to sustain new life.

"This earth is like my life. Parts of it are breaking down, never to return to the way they were before."

If only life would say to her, "Matilda, if you do this, this will happen. If you do the other, that will result." Instead the choices were murky as to which would, in the long run, provide the greater happiness or—conversely—the deeper sorrow.

"If I die today," she mused, "my only regret is that I lacked the courage to grab my heart's desire when he came to me."

Her jaw dropped. Did she really mean she'd weather society's barbs as a mistress?

She did.

She dug her hand into the soft earth, lifting a handful, and throwing it bit by bit into the brook.

"I fell in love at first sight. Those memories will stay with me until I draw my last breath."

With no effort on her part, she slipped once again into unconsciousness.

Chapter Thirty-Six

Geoff breathed in the night air of the forest heavily laden with dampness. The moist, soft soil along the pathway reminded him poignantly of Matilda. These generations of leaves broken down into soil were the breeding ground for her mushrooms. His heart twinged as he recalled her dirt-streaked face and her muddied hands holding the dull digging knife.

"There's the creek," Edrich called.

Geoff heard it, too, despite the considerable noise of the search party.

As they drew up to its embankment, he dismounted with a leap. It was too dark to see the bottom. He yelled for a torch and started down, calling Matilda's name and shouting for someone to accompany him.

"I'll come," Berwyn offered and started scrambling down behind him. "She'll need a friend."

William stayed on his horse.

Geoff worked his way partway down, torch in hand.

"There's no one," he called up. "She's not here."

He heard Berwyn say, "I'll go the rest of the way to make sure."

The torchlight bobbed lower, then out of sight. After searching for some time, she called back, "Nothing. Matilda's not here."

Geoff scrambled up the slope of the embankment. He vaulted over the edge and pulled Edrich from his horse.

"Where is she? Where is she?"

"I don't know," the kidnapper cried out, attempting to protect his body from the blows.

Geoff pushed him away. Edrich fell hard, unable to brace himself because his hands were tied. The baron turned to the tracker.

"Check the embankment to see if anyone besides the two of us disturbed the dirt there."

Jaelyn surveyed the ground carefully.

"No one was thrown down here. This is the wrong place."

Geoff became more desperate.

"Matilda can't be left in the cold and dark. At the mercy of the animals."

"We'll find her," Jaelyn said calmingly.

"Now what?" Berwyn asked.

"We'll go back until the dogs pick up the original scent," William said. "We'll try to discover where we went wrong."

"Start again?" Geoff could barely abide such a suggestion. He wanted results. He wanted them now.

"The idea has merit," Jaelyn said in a reasonable tone. "We backtrack slowly until the dogs find the horse's scent. We didn't follow the sign once we heard the creek."

Geoff remounted.

"Agreed."

The light wavered and flared as Jaelyn moved the torch from side to side, scrutinizing the vegetation for clues to Matilda's whereabouts. They traveled slowly along the trail until the dogs took off at an angle into the woods, yapping and scrambling through the brush.

"They found the scent," he shouted.

Chapter Thirty-Seven

Matilda emerged from the dense mental fog of semi-consciousness to barking. Terror awakened her fully from the strangling grip of blackness and pain. Wild dogs!

Pulling herself up, she groped for the stout branch she'd found earlier. Grasping it tightly, she looked about, preparing to do battle with the dogs as they appeared over the rim of the embankment. Straining to see through the foliage, she ignored the pain in her ankle and the damp cold. Only survival mattered. Discomfort must wait its turn.

From the sounds, the dogs were still some distance away and making no effort to come upon her stealthily. There seemed to be dozens of them. Matilda shivered, realizing what could happen, and fought to crush the panic welling up. She wouldn't become a meal without a fight.

She waited, heart pounding, wishing fervently she were at home, safe in her warm bed.

"If this day is to mark my end, so be it. I've had a loving family, good friends and Geoff."

Intense regret rippled through her at the loss of Geoff.

"If only…"

The baying of dogs dominated, but she now thought she heard horses' hooves and voices. She strained to filter through the myriad of muffled sounds. A search party!

"Help! Help! Help!"

Matilda called out time and again, her voice sounding increasingly panicked as each cry went unanswered.

"What if they pass me by?"

Exposure would kill her. She pinned her hopes on the dogs which—moments ago—she'd feared.

She dragged herself to the creek, her heart beating wildly, ignoring the agony of her leg. In the dim light of early dawn, she groped in the chill waters until she found two good-sized rocks. These she clanked together. The voices of the search party might drown her cries for help, but repeated rhythmic pounding would stand out from those sounds.

Sitting in the fast-running, cold water, she chose not to make herself comfortable by crawling out of the water. She feared—if she she halted the pounding—that would be just the moment the search party would pass her by.

Anxiety churned at her stomach. Her arms cramped and became increasingly weaker.

Although she couldn't pick out the words, she heard a blend of voices coming nearer. One horse crashed through the thick underbrush at a pace that would put it into the creek with her. The rider abruptly halted and dismounted. A new fear swept through her.

"Pray it's not bandits."

Matilda waited, her heart locked tight by uncertainty. Within seconds, the thick growth at the top of the embankment was rudely thrust aside. A torch lit the creek side and Geoff gazed down upon her, his face a mixture of wonder and shock.

"Matilda?"

He seemed bewildered, as if he couldn't imagine her sitting

there.

"Geoff!"

Her heart leapt with joy to see his dear face.

She waved to be sure he saw her in the dim light. She heard others arriving.

He shoved the torch at a villager and scrambled over the edge of the unstable embankment, his voice incredulous.

"You're alive!"

"I am," she replied with relief, "but probably not for much longer if you hadn't come."

"Blankets, ropes." He climbed hand-over-hand, grasping nearby roots to steady himself. Dirt dislodged by his descent rattled down the slope and splashed into the cold water.

"William is at the top waiting for you."

Her cousin called out, "I'm here, Matilda."

"I'm alive, William," she answered.

Shivers coursing through her damaged body mostly embodied relief, but they carried with them the knowledge that she'd come to a decision while she lay injured—she'd be Geoff's mistress. Her decision would hurt William.

"I'm here, too, Matilda," Berwyn yelled from above. "But this slope is too treacherous for me."

"I'm glad you're both near."

Geoff jumped the last few feet to the bottom and raced to her. He took her into a crushing embrace that gave no concern for her injury, but every concern for the healing of her heart. The embrace pinned her to him as if—by wrapping himself around her—he could fill her with the strength of his body.

He was leaning on her injured leg, causing protests of pain. Her ribs ached from the pressure, but she didn't want to end the moment. Indeed, a thread of disappointment wove through her when at last he released her.

"Let me get you out of this water."

"My right ankle is badly sprained."

"I'll protect it."

He put his cloak down on the drier ground and lifted her out of the stream. When he had her settled, he wrung out her wet clothing and wrapped the ends of his cloak around her shoulders, making sure it covered her entirely.

The warmth of the woolen cloth enveloping her made her want to fall asleep. She struggled to stay conscious. Drifting into a pleasant dream where she was safe and warm and loved was tempting, but she resisted. They needed her awake.

"Can you climb to the top with me?"

"I can't stand on my ankle."

"I'll get help."

Geoff ordered others to climb down to assist him. While they were doing so, he broke the branch Matilda had planned to use against the dogs into sections. He cut a strip from his tunic and wrapped this inadequate splint tightly to her leg.

"This will support your ankle when I move you. We can make something better when we get to the top."

"Last time, I patched you up. This time you patch me up."

Geoff kissed her—lingeringly—for all to see. The kiss sparked warmth that spread.

He reached out to trace the contours of her face with one finger.

"I was told you were dead."

"Seeing your dear face was like rising from the dead."

She shivered from the cold and from the realization of how

close she had come to death.

"Where's that rope? That blanket?" Geoff yelled. "We need some help here."

A rope—tied to a tree at the top—was thrown over the embankment and others soon followed. A blanket arrived next and Geoff quickly wrapped her in it.

Several young men climbed down and took charge of making harnesses. When they finished, Geoff slipped a harness over Matilda. Taking his time, he fastened it over her torso, his hands lingering here and there as he worked.

"We caught the man who did this to you. My sister paid him."

"Tomorrow I'll want to hear who and why," she said. "Today I only want to get out of here."

Geoff fastened her harness and attached his. With the help of two men, he lifted her as far up the slope as he could. Matilda clung to nearby roots with desperation.

"If I black out, I'll make this climb more difficult."

Geoff called out for others to take up the slack in his rope as he climbed higher. When braced, he pulled Matilda to him and held her while another man made his way up the slope and supported her on his shoulder until Geoff could reposition himself. In this way they inched slowly upwards as she bit her lip to keep from crying out with pain.

The searchers had cut the brush back from the embankment so Matilda could easily reach up for William's hand. As soon as she was near, he drew her the rest of the way over the rim and carried her to blankets spread on a bed of dried leaves.

"When I thought I would die, I made a decision, William. I must tell you."

Her voice trembled as she spoke.

"Let it wait, cousin, until you've rested."

He released her to Berwyn's care.

"You're soaked, my dear."

Berwyn had the peplos and the scarlet cloak brought and, under cover of blankets, Matilda awkwardly got out of her wet clothes and into dry clothing, ignoring the aches and pains. She listened as Geoff ordered half of the men to prepare to return to Caelfield with a team of dogs. They would carry news of the rescue.

Edrich, hands bound, would be dragged behind them. There would be no riding on his return trip. Berwyn would use his horse.

While her ankle was being braced and re-wrapped, Matilda ate the food Berwyn set out. William and Geoff hovered restlessly in the shadows. Impatient to unburden herself, Matilda beckoned to them and said what was in her heart.

"William, I love Geoff. I'll endure being mistress to be with him."

"I know, dear cousin. And he loves you as I loved my Aelswitha."

Matilda's heart soared.

He bent and kissed her tenderly on the forehead.

"I'll always cherish the cousin who brightened my life, but I release you from any obligations."

William—stepping out of her life as matter-of-factly as he had entered it—joined the early party heading back to Caelfield.

Geoff dropped to the earth beside her.

"Your cousin told me your secret. I offer not mistress, but wife—and my love for eternity. I vowed to God—if given a second chance—not king nor family nor anyone could keep me from

229

marrying you."

Joyful gladness danced in her heart. Wife!

Geoff grasped her hand tightly as if his very life depended on her answer.

"Do you love me and not my wealth?"

The answer was engravened on her heart. She'd gladly shout it to the world.

"It's you I love. I'd live with you even through poverty and disgrace."

Their kiss parted the heavens and all the blessings of the gods fell upon their love. Gathering her in his arms, he lifted her from the damp ground.

"Time to get you out of the cold."

He placed her onto his warhorse, being careful of her injured leg. He bounded up behind her, wrapping her scarlet cloak around them both.

As they made their way out of the ancient forest, Matilda saw trees bathed in the dawn of a new day. Dogs running freely were symbols of rescue, not fear. The damp that had been her enemy was now the earth's lifeblood. She looked onto the world with changed eyes, secure in the arms of her love.

She smiled.

The horse's hooves echoed the beat of her heart. In turn, her heart created a melody of its own. It sang a sweet refrain.

About the Author

JoAnn is a graduate of the University of California, Berkeley, with a double major in English and Social Science. She has her Masters in Teaching English from Fairleigh Dickinson University and her M.B.A. studies from Pepperdine University. She likes to walk, swim and read. She lives in Northern California.

To learn more, please visit www.joannsmithainsworth.com. Send an email to jsa@joannsmithainsworth.com.

GREAT
CHEAP
FUN

Discover eBooks!

THE FASTEST WAY TO GET THE HOTTEST NAMES

Get your favorite authors on your favorite reader, long before they're
out in print! Ebooks from Samhain go wherever you go, and work with
whatever you carry—Palm, PDF, Mobi, and more.

SAMHAIN
PUBLISHING
LTD

WWW.SAMHAINPUBLISHING.COM

Printed in the United States
219313BV00001B/69/P